NOT HERS TO POSSESS

NOT HERS TO POSSESS

RHONDA WEBSTER

SAPPHIRE BOOKS

SALINAS, CALIFORNIA

Editor - Tara Young
Cover Designer - Fineline Cover Design

Sapphire Books
Salinas, CA 93912
www.sapphirebooks.com

Printed in the United States of America
First Edition – March 2925

This and other Sapphire Books titles can be found
at
www.sapphirebooks.com

Dedication

This book is dedicated to the bravery of butch women, who are more visible than the rest of us and therefore are met with more criticism than those of us who often "pass" for straight. Sometimes I'm reminded of a cartoon where a dinosaur is looking at a person and telling a fellow dinosaur, "People are soft on the outside, but crunchy on the inside." I've learned that many butches are often hard looking on the outside but soft on the inside. Ah...you gotta love 'em!

Acknowledgement

No writer exists in a vacuum; we are blessed by friends and coworkers who help provide the material and kindly provide essential feedback.

I would like to thank my friend Sandra Pope, a very brave and loving woman, who was on the police force and from whom sprang up the fictitious Detective Persevere.

Thank you to my loving partner, Laura, a woman who also happens to be one of the most loving and brave women I

have ever known.

Chapter One: Breathing

Saturday, September 4

The comforter hung precariously off the bottom of the bed, and the sheets were in disarray. Morning rays of sunshine rode slowly across one wall; however, the two women were in comfortable unawareness of their surroundings.

"Oh...my...God!" Robin West said between ragged inhalations. "That...was wonderful! Why in the world...don't we...do this more often?" She wiped her short brown hair away from her brow, and her brown eyes shone brightly.

Bella Sanchez laughed cheerfully, though muffled by her pillow. Her long black hair cascaded around her head. In a useless attempt to bring back her energy, she inhaled deeply, then exhaled slowly. But it was no use. Her energy was gone...drained...spent. Being very still on the bed, she thought about breathing, for in each step of their tryst, there had been telltale breathing.

First came quiet, almost imperceptible breathing as she began to seduce her lover. These were careful, hopeful breaths of air, which slowly increased in measure. Then a sudden uptake of air that signaled the excitement of anticipation. It was a sign that Bella recognized, for it meant her seduction had met with success, and she had reason to expect there would be more to come. Still motionless, she allowed her body to press heavily into their bed as she stared at the ceiling.

It was white and blank, like the backdrop of a movie screen. Onto this imaginary screen, her mind replayed the wonderful lovemaking they had just shared.

Bella smiled, recalling when her own breathing had become sudden ragged breaths of intensity followed by a small series of little cries—whimpers, really—that had escaped her throat with the smallest emission of air. After that, a specific, very deep, and rapid inhalation, followed by an audible and prolonged release of breath, a precursor to the end of their lovemaking and the beginning of a bonding session. It was at these intimate moments in time when their breathing became calm and relaxed that she felt incredibly close to Robin. Now she calmly stared up at what she imagined was her white canvas—her slate of life—and felt that everything was clear and pure.

After sex, Bella noted that Robin's usually tense body was still and calm, and Robin's overactive mind tranquil and serene. Quietly, Bella listened to their peaceful, easy breathing until the next thing she knew, a tiny sob escaped her lips, and she was crying.

Robin turned and took Bella into her arms. She brushed a tear away, then kissed another.

"Are you okay?" she asked.

"Yes," Bella answered. "It was just so...intense! You know?"

Robin did know. She knew because her body was like Bella's; they were both women.

She knew because, occasionally, she also cried tears of release, tears that were devoid of sadness.

Robin licked her own lips, moistened by Bella's tears.

"Sweet and salty," Robin said. "Salty because they taste like the ocean and sweet... because they come from you." With those words, Robin tenderly brushed back Bella's hair and cradled Bella protectively in her arms. The two women sighed in unison, easy and gentle exhalations of togetherness.

When they finally felt capable of moving again, a bright beam of sunlight crept across the edge of their covers. Robin's wiry and light-skinned body wrapped around Bella's coffee-colored skin on a very feminine physique. Suddenly, the head of their rust-colored terrier popped into view, bobbing along as her front paws danced across the edge of the bed. Held in the dog's mouth was her pink leash.

"Is that supposed to be a hint?" Robin asked.

"Duh," Bella said to Rusty. "Sometimes moms can be kind of slow!"

"Not my fault," Robin said as she threw her arm heavily onto the bed. "Who can think?"

❧❧❧❧

As they dressed and then pulled on their shoes, the dog jumped up and down, panting with excitement. They would go for a walk, but it would not be a simple stroll through a local park like most people because Robin was not fond of crowded places. She avoided well-traveled paths in populated parks where leash laws were in effect, and she detested leash law enforcement officers. Robin was a free spirit and judging by their pet's body language when she was off leash, Rusty was in complete agreement. So, Bella was not surprised when Robin steered their car toward the local reservoir.

Robin parked her little truck near a ditch and at a right angle to a twelve-foot padlocked cattle-type gate. She turned off the ignition and grinned at Bella. The gate, which had a sign that clearly said, "No trespassing," led to unspoiled wilderness with a series of man-made lakes or water reservoirs that served the needs of Denver's water-greedy residents.

Bella knew that Robin's smile was heartfelt. Just behind the forbidding gate lay unspoiled beauty. Past the annoying signs and nuisance padlocks were sun-kissed land and wind-rippled water that existed in relative isolation.

They squeezed beneath a rusty chain that fastened the gate to a massive wooden fencepost. After breaching the gate, their feisty terrier bounded eagerly through tall grasses. Rusty would race ahead, double back to check on the progress of her humans, and then rush forward again. She needed little supervision because she knew the route well. As was their custom, the two women strode evenly along, while Rusty made frequent stops. Inhaling the aroma of grass and a hundred other delectable scents, Rusty twitched her nose, wagged her tail, and then took off at a dead run for the next scent marker along the way.

"Just think," Robin said, "that crazy mutt gets twice the exercise we do!"

Bella felt the warmth of the sun absorbed by her dark hair and listened to the sounds of nature that were theirs alone. She reached out and took Robin's hand, and the two of them gazed peacefully at the tall grass and trees before them. In unpopulated outdoor places, an act of being openly gay was a non-issue. Such was not the case, however, at Bella's job. While the majority of employees Bella worked with in human resources were open-minded about her sexuality, two workers out on the assembly line showed blatant homophobia.

Such disapproval caused Bella to vacillate in the open expression of her sexuality. One minute, she allowed Robin to hold her hand or kiss her in public; the next moment, she shied away.

Bella knew Robin wanted to protect her from homophobic backlash, but she was realistic enough to know that was impossible. Instead, Robin often settled for not being open in public and tried to be an available listener who would support Bella when the world turned cruel. But here, in the relative wilderness before them, there was nothing but the beauty of God's creation, and they felt free to be themselves.

Parting tall grass, they cautiously passed down a steep hillside and then turned toward the trickiest part of their adventure—the water crossing. The trick to crossing the stream without getting wet was to squeeze through a second locked gate, make a sharp left turn, and cross a makeshift bridge over the stream by balancing their way across the rounded top of a water pipe. The giant pipe crossed about three feet above the water's surface. On the left side of the pipe was a section of old field fencing interwoven with vines and overhanging tree limbs. The fence and limbs helped them with their balance, which became a bit unsteady whenever they stared down at the moving water. It was not a difficult crossing except for trying to guess which route their dog would take. Sometimes, Rusty waded across the shallow stream, but other times, she crowded them as she ran across the top of the pipe.

As Rusty hesitated, her owners carefully edged forward, then, without warning, their dog charged across the top of the pipe with both women directly in her path. Bella saw her first and was able to back safely onto the grass. However, Robin, who was farther out, stepped as far off to one side as possible, which Rusty decided was a signal for her to pass. So, instead of simply slowing her pace and following her owner, Rusty made the mistake of moving to the edge of the pipe. Without the advantage of hands to reach out and grab an available tree limb, the dog's left front paw suddenly slid down the side of the pipe and between the old fencing. Rusty yelped, regained her balance, jumped in front of Robin, and then ran the rest of the way across, leaving behind a small trail of blood.

Pointing at the blood, Robin said, "Oh, no! She's hurt!"

"We'd better get over there and see what happened," Bella said.

They rushed to the opposite side of the stream where Rusty was furiously licking her paw. Between the two women, Bella had no question who would take charge. Robin was an experienced nurse, and Rusty was originally her dog. She was the one with first-aid training and had routinely seen a great deal of blood. Bella was certain that Robin would know exactly what to do.

Kneeling over, Robin pulled up a paw to take a look. "Oh, my God!" she said. "Look!"

Not only was one of the dog's toenails ripped completely off, but the inner meaty part of the nail, known as the quick, was dangling from her foot.

"Geez…that must hurt!" Robin said.

The dog turned her head to look at Robin with her large almond-colored eyes. She made a tiny whimper, and Robin let go of Rusty and reeled backward with a twisting motion. She crumpled to the ground, barely managing to keep her face out of the dirt.

"Everything…is…spinning!" Robin said. "Oh,

man, I think I'm gonna puke!"

Standing beside her, Bella moved forward and patted Robin on the back. "It's okay. Just keep your head down for a minute." Robin continued kneeling.

"Now I'm gonna pick up our girl," Bella said, "but don't look! Okay?"

With that, Bella knelt over the dog, wrapped Rusty's paw in a napkin from her pocket, and scooped her into her arms.

Regaining the color in her face, Robin slowly got to her feet. It was a tad amusing for Bella to occasionally glimpse weakness in her extremely self-sufficient can-do-anything woman.

However, when she looked into Robin's eyes, she noted that her gaze was locked on her T-shirt.

Looking down, she noted a streak of Rusty's blood across the front of her blouse.

"Don't look!" she repeated more forcefully. Robin obeyed, turning away again. "Oh, man, how embarrassing! I can't believe I just did that!" "Honey, you're human," Bella said, "that's all.

Bella carried Rusty across the stream, up the hill, and all the way to the car with Robin trailing behind. It was a steep hill, and the dog was a solid little bundle, but Bella didn't complain. With Rusty cradled in Bella's arms, Robin took charge of driving them to the vet.

When the receptionist called them back, Bella kindly left Robin alone in the waiting room. The vet trimmed off the exposed tissue and put a dressing on it. From the vet's demeanor, it was clear that this awful-looking injury was a minor and ordinary event.

Human Resources
Saturday, September 4

Bella was at work typing at her computer when she heard a man up front shouting at Ester, who was her prim and older coworker.

"I've been here for four months!" the man said. "I was supposed to be covered a month ago! Now the hospital told me I don't have any health insurance!"

Bella listened as Ester assured the man that she would check it out. A minute or two of calmness followed, and then the quiet was pierced by the man's voice.

"I what?" the man yelled. "I damn well better have insurance 'cause my wife's down there at that thousand-dollar-a-day hospital, and my butt's on the line!"

Bella pushed back from her computer and started toward the front counter to lend moral support to Ester. As she made her way there, the man said, "Clerical error, my ass! The hospital made me sign that I would be financially responsible. And I did sign because I had to. My wife was sick, and I knew I had insurance. But God damn it, if you all fucked it up, I'm screwed...I'm screwed big-time!"

Bella watched as the color left Ester's face, and she backed away from the counter.

"Sir, I will not be subjected to profanity!" Ester informed him.

Bella suppressed a smile because her friends routinely used the same profanity that had clearly upset Ester. She then stepped halfway in front of her.

"I'll take care of this, Ester," she said calmly.

The man turned his attention from Ester to Bella. Clearly, Bella was much younger than Ester, and as the man glanced from one woman to the other, a look of suspicion crossed his face.

"Are you the manager?" he asked.

"Yes," she lied.

Without another word, Ester retreated to the back.

"Whatever is wrong, I personally apologize to you, sir," Bella said. "And I promise you that I will fix it."

"Well…what the hell happened?" he asked. "I'll find out for you. May I see your insurance card?" He pushed the card forward on the counter.

"Okay, Mr. Thompson, you say you've been working here for four months?" she asked.

"Yes."

"And you're full time?"

"Yes."

"Well then, you're right, you are supposed to be covered. Let me call over there and straighten this out." Bella then moved closer to the angry man.

"What happened to your wife?" she asked quietly.

"They don't know," he said. His well-chiseled face suddenly turned a beefy red. "Female problems!" he stammered uncomfortably.

"Is she at Denver Memorial?"

"Yes."

"I know people who work there, and they have good doctors and nurses. Don't worry, they'll take good care of her. There's coffee over there. Help yourself while I get this mess untangled for you."

Bella picked up the phone and gave a woman his identification number. After that, the woman placed her on hold. The music was soft rock, which was a step up from the usual elevator music. To nothing but the sound of the background music, and solely for the benefit of the distraught workman, Bella talked into the unmanned phone. First, she asked for a manager, and then she relayed the problems that Mr. Thompson was experiencing. Sternly, she told the blank phone line that this man was entitled to health insurance and that someone had better fix it right away.

Mr. Thompson sipped on his coffee, satisfied that she was going up the ranks to the very top.

Ten minutes later when Bella finally solved what turned out to be a simple clerical error and Mr. Thompson calmly left their office, Ester slapped a handmade "Manager" sign onto Bella's computer, and the two of them shared a good laugh.

⁂

Bella never knew exactly when Robin would get home from her three-to-eleven shift at Denver Memorial Hospital, but whatever time it was, she wanted to be ready for her when she finally walked in the door. While bathing herself in a lavender-scented bubble bath, her thoughts drifted to lustful desires and an urgency to be pulled into Robin's arms.

At that very moment, Robin was cruising through the lonely night, praying that Bella would still be awake. At the same time Bella was running a washrag over her mocha-colored skin, Robin was creating a dominant fantasy in her mind.

Robin had once explained to Bella that she didn't know why she always wanted to play the sexually assertive partner in her relationships. They both knew she was not a short woman who needed an ego boost; at 5'8", she was slightly taller than most women. Nor did she feel powerless in her career since her job as a registered nurse was an autonomous position. Although she was a child who had received less nurturing than she wanted, she had never been molested or unwanted or unloved.

However, Robin confessed that she did prefer being assertive and loved to think that the initiation of sex was her idea, even when it wasn't. Fortunately, Robin's assertive sexual behavior was not problematic in their relationship because Bella was pleased to be passive. She was confident enough in her own sexuality that occasionally she even teased Robin into being on the receiving end of their encounters.

After sex, Robin often smiled with a self-satisfied smugness, saying she felt that their sexual encounter drew them closer together. Yet she was occasionally bothered by the belief that she was a sexist of the highest order because in her mind sexual domination was another form of oppressing women. To her way of thinking, since sexual oppression was politically incorrect, her preference to dominate was unacceptable. She confessed to Bella that if they had a truly healthy relationship, they should take equal turns in their sexual encounters, just as they did in every other aspect of their lives, but being passive was not much of a turn-on for her.

In these moments of uncertainty, Bella recognized the crack in Robin's reserve and took full advantage of it by getting Robin to consent to passive lovemaking. Bella noticed that when Robin allowed herself to be passive, although she claimed it offered a sort of relaxed freedom, she seldom reached the same state of arousal as she did when she was assertive.

Lying back in her bathtub, Bella summoned a shadowy image of Robin's tall torso with wide shoulders, long arms, and small breasts, a build common to swimmers. Bella watched flickers of candlelight dance along the shiny edges of her reflective tub.

"Darling," Bella's voice echoed in the white tiled bathroom, "when are you coming home?" In answer, the wind of the late fall evening teased falling leaves against the windowpane.

The First Time They Met
Saturday, September 4

After she toweled off and carried her scented candles to the coffee table, Bella sat alone in their dimly lit living room and watched the shadows of tree limbs dance across the walls. She crossed her arms and buried her fingers into the deep pile fabric of her soft robe, hugging herself and thinking longingly about Robin. With fondness, she recalled their first contact.

Bella had been searching through lesbian singles ads, scanning mostly in jest. She noted the usual odd assortment of ads—too brief or nothing but a single come-on line followed by ads bitching about game players. However, a handful were refreshingly different. The ones she found most interesting were undoubtedly written by women who were honest and appealing. Robin's ad struck Bella as blatantly honest.

Robin openly admitted faults, which to Bella, seemed odd, as this would undoubtedly cause many seekers to pass her by, to which Robin responded, "That was my intention, to allow certain women to reject me immediately." She told Bella that early rejection was far less time-consuming and painful than the way in which she had previously managed her life. Three bad mismatches had not only been painful, but also costly.

Although Robin admitted she didn't like living alone and even believed that she suffered from loneliness, she said she knew that sometimes she needed it. Even after it was clear to Bella that the two of them were quite compatible, Robin continued to insist they wait a minimum of six months before moving in together. Robin could not escape the fear that she might repeat the same mistakes all over again.

They had moved in together seven years ago… seven years! It hardly seemed possible!

Their time together had flown by all too fast.

Bella leaned back on the couch and sighed. She had quickly fallen head over heels in love with Robin, and even now, she knew without a doubt that she was still in love with her.

Robin made her laugh and kept their life interesting. Although Robin had a slightly butch side and claimed that she was not comfortable being called "sweet," she had a child-like sweetness that she often found touching, particularly with animals.

As explanation for Robin's often keyed-up hyperactive behavior, Robin told her she had been diagnosed late in life with attention deficit disorder, (specifically, Attention Deficit/ Hyperactivity Disorder). The worst ADHD crisis periods came about when Robin suddenly found herself living alone. She found organization problematic, she was unable to keep up with her mail, she had great difficulty keeping appointments, and she seldom finished projects. Outside of a slow-cooking crock pot and a microwave oven, which thankfully turned itself off, Robin's wandering attention caused her to burn most food she tried to cook.

As Bella came to know her, she decided that Robin

was cursed with impulsiveness from two dissimilar sources; besides ADHD, she also had the astrological sign of the mercurial Gemini.

Robin told Bella that although being impulsive led to fun experiences, it also led her into disastrous personal relationships, which she later attributed to leaping in much too fast. It was for this reason that she created the long ad that inspired one respondent to tell Robin that she "said too much."

Counseling had helped Robin better understand her relationship misconceptions. She learned that up to that point in her life, she had looked for rigidly organized partners whom she mistakenly believed could help bring her chaotic life to a semblance of order. Unfortunately, supremely organized people tended to be inflexible to the point that they were unable to tolerate living with someone like Robin, their free-thinking and unorganized opposite.

For example, Robin's behavior in stores seemed particularly problematic to inflexible partners because they believed it was an unspoken duty of Robin's to stand patiently and obediently in line next to them. So when they looked around and discovered that Robin had once again wandered out of sight, they invariably became exasperated.

Bella, however, did not see the point of fighting a person's basic nature. She didn't get angry when Robin wandered off; she gave her permission to wander. And over their years together, Bella continued to give such permission, even though it meant that she was left standing in line alone. Utilizing the modern magic of a cellphone, when she was ready to go, Bella called Robin, and Robin reappeared.

The career of nursing seemed a good fit for a

person with ADD because it was an active and diverse job that involved running around. As a nurse, she seldom had to stick with one specific task or to remain in a particular place for long. Nursing was a profession that constantly challenged Robin's body and her mind.

When Bella thought about the statement that opposites attract, she realized that opposite characteristics could be complementary. Robin was a talker and Bella a listener. Robin loved to write, and Bella loved to read. And their household functioned better, too, because Robin was a good mechanic and Bella a much better cook. While Robin was a disaster at handling mail and the checkbook, Bella was adept at such tasks. As for their sexual appetites, happily, Bella thought these areas compatible, as well. Bella was earthy; Robin was flighty. Robin told her friends that Bella kept her pleasantly grounded.

Upon hearing the arrival of Robin's truck, Bella quickly pushed play on the DVD player and pretended that the movie flickering on the screen was foremost on her mind. Straining over the sounds of the movie, she heard Robin's familiar voice in the kitchen.

"Hi, Rusty! Boy, I'm glad to be home. Where's your sexy momma?"

Robin patted her excited terrier on the head, grabbed a fresh baked cookie off the counter, and hurried toward Bella with long strides. "Hi, Bell."

"I made you cookies," Bella said, then smiled when she noticed Robin holding a partially eaten cookie.

"They're good!" Robin looked at the television set. "What are you watching? Uh…is that what I think it is?"

Bella grinned sheepishly.

"How could you?" Robin demanded in a teasing voice. "How could you watch a sexy lesbian movie without me?"

Bella laughed. "I can rewind," she said quickly.

Robin pushed her short brown hair away from her face, flopped onto the loveseat beside Bella, and kissed her excitedly.

"First, I want to tell you about what happened at work today. Do you remember the young man in a coma that I've been telling you about? Well, guess what? He woke up today!

Everyone was so happy that we cried…even grouchy old Irma!"

In a voice giddy with excitement, she related the miraculous recovery of her patient. The young man had been her patient for weeks on end, and as time passed without improvement, his prognosis had turned grim. Pessimistically, they feared that he was another helmetless motorcycle crash victim on his way toward becoming a vegetable.

During the expression of her heartfelt emotion, Bella watched as Robin valiantly tried to fight back tears. Sensing that Robin needed an outlet for her emotion, Bella encouraged such outward displays. Bella noticed that when she turned her full attention toward Robin, her macho posturing often melted away.

When Robin finished relating the evening's event, Bella gave her a hug. "That's great!

I'm happy for all of you!'

Then she told Robin that although her experience of the day was not as life-altering, she also had a happy event. She then described her conversation with the irate man with no insurance. She explained how she was able to help straighten out the mess for the anxious husband so he could stop worrying and return to his ailing wife's bedside.

"I'm proud of you," Robin said. "Isn't it wonderful to have a positive effect on the lives of other people?"

When they finished sharing their day's events, Bella started the movie from the beginning. Seemingly mesmerized by lesbian actors, Robin's body visibly began to relax and unwind as the story unfolded before them. When the movie ended, Bella felt Robin's right hand gently exploring her palm and noticed Robin's gaze roving across her body like a predator…aroused and hopeful. Bella smiled. To her, watching a sexy lesbian movie was like preheating an oven. Even better, the movie about the intimate aspects of lesbianism helped them both become sexually responsive at the same time.

Turning toward her, Robin took Bella's face into her hands and kissed her lightly on her forehead. Cradling her head in her hands like a cherished jewel, she gently kissed both eyelids. She brushed her lips tenderly across Bella's face, then pulled back and gazed into her eyes. I know you,, I cherish you, and I love you, said her eyes. Then Robin's lips found Bella's. Warmth against warmth and softness against softness. Straddling Bella on the sofa, Robin kissed her lightly on the lips. At first, they were kisses of familiar intimacy and genuine affection, tentative and playful. But in response, Bella knew that her own lips were soft, warm, and yielding. In recognition of her willingness, she heard Robin's soft, almost surprised intake of air.

Robin often teased Bella about being sexually easy. Honey, she'd often said, I think you're usually sitting on go.

Grabbing a fistful of the short dark hair at the

base of Bella's head, Robin eagerly drew her lover toward her. As she did so, her other hand on the side of Bella's neck brushed against her pounding pulse. Soon they were kissing like sex-starved lovers. Emboldened by Bella's responses, Robin pushed her thigh firmly against Bella's body and began rocking with a gentle insistence.

After sensuous rocking pressure with her thigh, Robin used her right hand to caress her body from outside Bella's silky pajama bottoms. Then, ever so lightly, she ran her fingers up her inner thigh, changed direction, and rubbed in large circles, playfully avoiding the inner and most sexually responsive portions of Bella's body.

Bella briefly pulled away and then moved her body back toward Robin's roaming fingers. She reached out and pulled forward on the back of Robin's neck. Without a word, Robin stood and smiled. She pulled Bella to a standing position, wrapped both arms around her, and kissed her passionately. Robin brought her arms around Bella's waist, untied her robe, and ran her fingers lovingly beneath its plush surface. Bella had a distinctly female body with large breasts, a trim waist, and curvaceous hips. Robin grasped her hand and drew her toward their bedroom.

Bella allowed herself to be led. However, Robin stopped them short before they reached the bed, suddenly grasping Bella's upper arms with a firm grip. Spinning around, Robin used her entire body to pin Bella against the solid oak closet door. The door settled against the doorjamb yet held firm.

Bella melted into her without resistance. Robin's right thigh pressed rhythmically into her warmth, causing the door to rattle with their movements.

The noisiness of their lovemaking didn't worry them because no one was around to hear their intimate escapade except for their dog, and Rusty was so familiar with the sounds they made that her reaction was to curl herself into a ball and sigh heavily.

The women's lips pressed together. Robin's tongue darted into Bella's warm mouth.

Providing a strong thigh for her to ride on, Robin ran one hand firmly over Bella's rounded hips. Her fingertips found the waistband of Bella's silk pajama bottoms, slipped under it, and eased the fabric downward.

Bella smiled to herself. There's nothing like being kissed, petted, and having my lover slowly make her way across my body. Robin's hand moved downward where she lightly ran the tips of two fingers over the inner part of pajama bottoms that covered the warmest and most intimate part of her body.

When Bella's entire body helplessly slid down the door, Robin lifted her up and eased her onto their bed. As Robin hurriedly slipped out of her nursing uniform, Bella lay back and watched. Smiling, Robin turned and peeled off Bella's pajama bottoms so she could run the palms of her hands over her bare curvaceous thighs. Bella was used to Robin undressing her and had made it easy to push aside the plush robe to expose her ample breasts.

Their sexual communication was incredibly good. Robin knew Bella loved foreplay. She enjoyed a lengthy period of being kissed and caressed before being physically entered, and Bella soaked up the thoughtful attentions of a lover who so earnestly wanted to please. Patiently, Robin teased and stroked Bella's warm skin, making her way across Bella's body as a woman who loved and cherished every square inch of flesh. Her slow and gentle foreplay succeeded in stimulating Bella into a frenzy of sexual desire. Yet Robin did not ease up. She yearned to encourage and draw out a heightened sense of anticipation, and best of all, she had the skills to do so.

Even though Bella's ardent responses clearly showed her readiness, Robin wickedly continued to make her wait. She fondled Bella's breasts, then suckled, nibbled, and toyed with her nipples, until her anticipation was drawn out. When Robin finally allowed her fingers to slowly glide across Bella's intimate slippery surfaces, her measured movements remained unhurried. Despite her building excitement, Robin paced herself, drawing out the anticipation. Repeatedly, her fingers circled, skated, and toyed with her without entering. Finally, when it seemed she could take it no more, Bella groaned. When it came to making her woman wait, Robin bordered on cruelty.

"Please," Bella said.

"Please?" Robin mocked her.

Bella groaned again.

"Please what?" Robin asked, taunting her.

"Please," Bella pleaded. "Please go inside me!"

In a deep and quiet tone, Robin pressed her lips near Bella's ear and asked, "Do you want me?"

"Yes, yes, I want you! Please!"

Then, and only then, did Robin's fingers plunge inside her, deep inside, hooking upward as she slid in, then pulling back and repeating the motion. At the same time, Bella could feel Robin use her tongue to stimulate the area just above the movements of her busy fingers.

Bella responded by thrusting her hips up and

down: two bodies moving together. Robin knew what she wanted and needed. Bella's excitement climbed, higher and higher still, until finally she collapsed onto the bed in a delicious wave of internal release.

Raining tiny kisses on her forehead, Robin then crawled upward and drew Bella into her protective arms, cradling her until Bella's body slowly transitioned from excited and tense to spent and satiated. Usually, at this time, it was Robin's turn. However, to Bella's surprise, Robin said that tonight, all she wanted was to allow the woman she loved to lie perfectly still in her arms and to enjoy their closeness.

Chapter Two: Birdseed

Saturday, September 4

With aviator sunglasses and short cropped brown hair, Salvia Singleton looked the part of a handsome young man as she drove her royal blue Jeep slowly westward, patiently waiting at red lights and taking her sweet time to reach her destination. Acting leisurely around her mother was not a freedom to which she was accustomed. In fact, her mother's demanding and impatient attitude had made Salvia's life a living hell. Her desire for her mother to mellow in her old age had been wishful thinking; Salvia had not been that lucky.

The sorriest and longest-lasting heartache between the two women was the fact that Salvia was born a girl. Her mother wanted a boy, but after Salvia was born, her mother discovered she was unable to have any more children. Had the woman been the slightest bit reasonable, she would have settled for what she got because Sal was more masculine than most men turned out to be. Her daughter was so strong that she easily managed all her mother's lifting requests. She also loved tools, was handy with them, and used them to keep everything in her mother's house in good working order.

Unfortunately, her mother couldn't be pleased. Although she was the one who encouraged the masculinization of her daughter, it was not unusual for her to belittle her daughter's boyish appearance. The older woman often bemoaned the fact that she was never going to get any grandsons if Salvia didn't change her ways and begin to attract men.

Men, men, men! Sal had never understood why such single-minded and often foolish creatures were an object of desire to her mother because men were certainly of no interest to her.

"You were right about one thing, Mother," Sal muttered toward her windshield. "You are never going to get any grandchildren…male or female!"

The metallic paint of the well-polished Jeep reflected brightly in the sunlight. The handsome young woman steered her vehicle between two stone columns and glided quietly down the wide lane of Peaceful Slumber Cemetery in Lakewood, Colorado.

"P 124," she said to herself as she turned left. She tossed her sunglasses on the light denim-colored seat and stepped into partially shaded sunlight with a bag in hand. Like most cemeteries, the grass was a weed-free healthy shade of green and shaded by well-tended trees. In the distance was an old section, adorned with a variety of headstones. With purposeful strides, clad in her usual brown leather boots and blue jeans, Salvia headed for the new section, the one with ground-level headstones, or markers as they called them, which were low maintenance. Even though she disliked them, Sal had to admit that since her mother had never been low maintenance before, she was certainly past due.

Salvia stopped at the newest grave, bent her head down, and began a one-sided conversation.

"Hi, Mother It's beautiful here. You'd like the big tree that's on the hill. I got you a nice grave marker, too." Then she stood quietly, listening to the silence.

This was not the type of conversation she had grown accustomed to. Her overbearing mother had taken over every interaction of her life. Her mother was the one who talked. Sal listened.

"A stroke," she said. "It happened so fast that I didn't even get a chance to say goodbye.

But at least you didn't suffer."

Then in the silence that followed, Salvia's polite façade began to wear away. Suddenly, she found a new opportunity, the freedom to utter words she had never dared to speak.

"Why, Mother?" Salvia suddenly blurted out. "Why didn't you love me?"

Her blue eyes were piercing. Tears welled up and threatened to spill over. She scanned the immediate area of the cemetery, relieved to note that no one else was around.

"I did everything for you! But no one could please you, could they? I tried to be the son you never had! So why couldn't you have at least been kind to me? Why couldn't you let yourself love me? Was I that unlovable?"

Salvia began to cry, tears she knew were not for her mother, but for herself, because a part of Sal feared that she really might be unlovable. Then anger welled up inside her until this stronger emotion replaced her self-pity. The truth was, Salvia had enough self-awareness to recognize that most of the negative feelings she had about herself were the direct result of the relationship with her mother.

A noisy motor briefly interrupted her thoughts. Salvia looked up from her mother's gravesite and saw a groundskeeper cruising by in a John Deere four-wheel drive vehicle. She started to turn her head away to hide her tear-streaked face until the irony of the moment struck her.

The caretaker, if he saw her at all, would think she was grieving the loss of her mother. He would assume she was paying a normal visit with the anticipation of more to come. He didn't know her tears were born of anger, frustration, and relief. He had no way of knowing this was her first visit since the funeral, over two weeks ago, nor that Salvia decided this would be the last.

Patiently, she waited for the man to pass by. Then she savagely threw down a dying rose that she had carried clenched in her right hand. "This half-dead rose is for the half-dead feelings I have for you!"

Salvia stood, glaring at the withered rose on the ground and squeezing a bag of birdseed.

"And you know how you wanted perpetual care, Mother?" Sal asked. "Well, you're not getting it! In fact, I'm gonna tell you the real reason I even showed up today. You see, I brought some birdseed. Yeah, you heard me right, I said birdseed. It's for the party."

The stocky young woman tore open the plastic bag of birdseed and scattered it all over the gravesite, paying particular attention to generously cover the marking stone. Tiny golden balls of seed bounced on the slick surface of the stone, then came to rest, covering the marker's background and half of the raised lettering.

"Do you know what happens when you put down birdseed?" Salvia waited. No one answered. "Gee, this silence is nice," she said, her voice dripping with sarcasm.

Salvia scanned over a long row of discrete markers and focused on the trunks of stately oak trees where two squirrels were playing tag.

"Well, I'll tell you," Salvia continued. "The squirrels and the birds will come down from the trees and have a party. See, they'll be happy, even if you never were. They'll gobble up all this bird seed until their little bellies are full, and then they'll piss and shit all over your grave! Canada geese might come by, too. They always leave a real mess. And guess what? I won't be back to clean it up, either!"

Salvia looked at the seed, considering the consequences.

"Of course," she said thoughtfully, "the little critters won't be able to find every single seed. The uneaten ones will slip into the grass and down into the loose dirt around the edges of the gravestone. Eventually, they'll spring up and grow into a bunch of ugly old weeds, all around the edges of your grave marker. And my poor back sure knows how much you hate weeds. But perpetual weeds are what you deserve, and perpetual weeds are what you're gonna get! So stew in it, Mother! Do you hear me?"

Salvia turned and took two steps toward her Jeep, then spun back around in the fallen leaves. "Oh, and one last thing. I just hope, wherever the hell you wind up, that you don't suck the happiness out of anyone else like you did to me!"

Looking back over at the two squirrels whose curious brown eyes were now staring cautiously at her from their tree trunk, Salvia said her last words to her mother.

"Let the party begin!" With that, Salvia Singleton turned and headed toward her Jeep.

She did not look back.

Chapter Three: Salvia's New Direction

Friday, September 10

Being task-oriented, Salvia moved through the various phases of her mother's death with relative ease. Up until the birdseed incident, she had continued her regimented life as if her mother still reigned. But the graveside visit became a turning point in her life. No longer did she tiptoe around her own house. She now stomped across rooms, slammed doors, and sometimes, when ridiculously stupid commercials blared from her mother's old television set, she even bellowed across the room at them. Finally, on a whim, she decided it was time to make the house her own.

Salvia boxed up the ugly knickknacks her mother had made, along with other worthless ornaments bought at senior arts and crafts bazaars. Into the garbage she threw sickly smelling mothballs stored in the back hallway, along with her mother's fancy damn window sheers that blocked out entirely too much sunlight. What is the purpose of a window if you're going to cover it up? Carefully reading the labels on her mother's prescription bottles, Sal saved the pain medications, sleeping pills, and tranquilizers. However, she threw out all the antibiotics, heart medication, and water pills.

For a moment or two, she considered having one hell of a big bonfire with all her mother's discarded belongings, but then Salvia's practical side took over, and she patiently boxed the belongings up. It would be wrong to throw away items that other people can use. She filled boxes with her mother's clothing, purses, shoes, and jewelry and dropped them at the Salvation Army. As for her mother's old recliner, it was no easy task for a single person to do, but she managed to drag it outside, where she stuck a "Free" sign on the faded material. Then she jumped into her Jeep and steered toward the shopping center.

Salvia bought herself a new La-Z-Boy recliner, two colorful throw rugs, and a cordless telephone, which included an answering machine. She was particularly proud of the answering machine because it was an appliance her mother had adamantly refused to have in her house.

Once Salvia had freed her purchases from their packaging and carefully placed these latest items around the house, she sat back and studied the results of her home decorating. These were good changes, differences that served to update the place. It was her house now, and after all these years of living there, it was finally starting to look and feel that way.

Sal twisted the cap off a bottle of beer and took a big swallow. Drinking alcohol was just one more thing her mother had not allowed. At the age of thirty-two, she thought it was pathetic that her mother had to die before Salvia was free to do as she pleased.

At first, the effects of the beer felt pleasant. The alcohol relaxed her body and her mind.

Instead of being concerned with the usual thoughts of what her mother might think or desire,

Salvia experienced the heady freedom of seriously considering what she—Salvia

Singleton—wanted in life. But the problem

with entertaining such thoughts was that it caused her to dwell on her loneliness. What I really need is a companion, a lover. I need a woman to bring laughter and joy into my life.

Over the years, Salvia had experienced three accidental and very secretive lesbian relationships, but they were of short duration. She didn't know if this was because they were mismatched to begin with or if the women didn't find her personality attractive. However, she thought it more likely that the relationship with her mother was to blame. The ridiculous restrictions her mother placed on every aspect of her life had undoubtedly been detrimental to her brief and hidden relationships.

Dealing with her mother's tyranny and jealousy had even made friendships difficult. In the end, it had been easier not to make any attempts toward building relationships. However, now that she was free to pursue whomever she wanted, Salvia floundered with inexperience. She didn't know how to go about meeting women.

With unlimited time to think about it, Salvia studied her options. She could meet women on the internet, but she was not familiar with cyberspace and didn't trust it. Also, she was a poor speller and a two-fingered typist. That left softball and gay bars. Unfortunately, the softball season was ending. So, she drew on her inner courage and decided to prowl the lesbian bars.

Having never given thought to it before, Salvia now considered it a pity that she had no friends to give her pointers and support. Nor did she believe that any how-to manuals existed for butches like her who desperately needed advice about how to meet women.

More specifically, she wished for a manual about how to pick up one single woman because Sal was not a player nor was she a greedy person. Salvia was strictly monogamous.

❧❧❧❧

Salvia began her quest in an upscale lesbian bar that younger women frequented. She had to consume one bottle of beer to get inside the door and two more bottles of the same liquid courage to make a move. Even then, her first interaction was merely to play a game or two of pool. By the time she got to the pool table, she was a little too tipsy to play the game well. Besides, the only women willing to play with her were also butch, and in her mind, a femme would fit better in her life.

Finally screwing up her courage, Salvia forced herself to ask three women to dance. When all three women politely turned her down, she retreated to a corner to lick her wounds and analyze her performance. Had she come on too strong? She didn't think she did. Was there something wrong with her looks? If Salvia knew anything, she knew that she was okay in the looks department, average, with a leaning toward handsome. Her hair was plain brown but had a healthy shine to it. She'd always had a nice complexion, her blue eyes were piercing, and her teeth clean, white, and straight. She was a tad stocky but mostly muscular. Are they all in relationships? Then she forced herself to try again.

❧❧❧❧

Saturday, September 11

Careful to remain more sober on her next time at the bar, Salvia only asked women to dance who were standing or sitting alone. But again, she received nothing but refusals. Salvia headed for home, alone and dejected. She wondered if women were this mean to men. Judging from what she had seen in the past, she concluded that women were even worse to men. At least all the refusals she received were polite. She didn't hear any of the women laughing at her with their friends, and that—she knew—sometimes did happen to men.

This gave Salvia a new perspective on the life of men. Sal had often wondered why she had seen men so shy that they passed up opportunities that would have worked out well for them.

Now she knew that this undoubtedly was one of the reasons because approaching a woman was much harder than it looked.

At last, Salvia went home and spent the next week rethinking her strategy. She tried to see herself as she might appear to others. She had overheard women describe her as a soft butch. The bar she frequented was more of an upscale kind of place with less role playing. But there was talk of an older and smaller bar named The Side Door whose clients were blue-collar women. So she promised herself, come next Friday, that she would give The Side Door a try.

❧❧❧❧

Monday, September 13

In the meantime, Salvia focused all her attention

on her job at an auto parts store. She had worked her way up from counter help to assistant manager. She had befriended male coworkers and was a quick study on car parts. According to rumor, they were building a new and larger store in the area, and Sal's manager, a guy named Jake, planned to take over that position. The general assumption was that Salvia would then be promoted to his position at the current location. God knew, as a faithful employee of eight years, she certainly deserved it.

When she arrived at work that day, she immediately noticed a new addition to the staff, a pimple-faced young man named Aaron. She also noted that Jake was keeping a close eye on this boy, whose every action appeared to meet with his approval. She soon learned that he was Jake's son. Worse, her boss avoided Salvia, and by that afternoon, she overheard two of her coworkers guessing that Aaron was being groomed for the job that, by all rights, should be hers.

"You know," Salvia said to Jake later that day, "I've been waiting a long time for a promotion."

But Jake cut her off and appeared to perform a verbal tap dance, first smoothly praising Salvia's past performance and then, in a harsher voice, denying that he would ever be unfair to her. Yet Salvia noticed that he carefully avoided making any promises.

❧❧❧❧

Wednesday, September 16

Two days later, Jake claimed that the company was reorganizing. He said Aaron and Salvia had to be laid off. Her coworkers flatly told her that this was

Jake's thinly disguised plan to rid himself of Salvia, so that he could groom Aaron for the manager position. And even Salvia had to admit that such a plan would go easier once she was out of the way. If Jake had that in mind, this would be blatantly unfair, but she felt incapable of fighting it.

In the back of her mind, she envisioned becoming the manager at one of their other local chain stores, and a good word from Jake could be important to her. She did not dare release the anger she felt for the injustice done to her. She merely bottled up her resentment.

However, losing her job was a stunning blow. One minute, Salvia had work friends and a steady job. The next minute, she lost a great deal of her life—her stable schedule, productive work hours, a decent income, and time that was mercifully filled. More importantly, she lost her sense of belonging. Sal was a person who liked to be useful. In the blink of an eye, she was stripped of her camaraderie and her usefulness.

Naturally, Salvia wanted to yell at someone, but there was no one to yell at. She decided the best solution was to apply for a job at the two other chain stores in town. So, the next day, in a painstakingly slow manner, she typed out a résumé and headed out the door. At the first store, she was given a noticeably short interview. She thought the manager seemed distant but chalked it up to her imagination. He was the same man she had talked to on multiple occasions in the past about work-related subjects, and in those instances, they had gotten along fine. However, it was not her imagination that the second manager was uncomfortable as he spoke to her. He emphatically told her he didn't have an opening at the present time, nor did he expect a manager's position to become available.

"What the hell is going on?" Salvia asked herself. "Why am I getting the brush-off?"

She had always had a reputation as a solid employee with the company, or at least that was how things used to be. She was walking out of the second auto parts store when she spotted Bill, a former coworker. She took advantage of the opportunity by pressing him for an answer. Reluctantly, Bill admitted that Jake rehired Aaron four days later. According to Bill, two employees told Jake that Salvia may have a legitimate claim against him for his unfair actions, and the man had reacted by badmouthing Salvia to the managers at the other chain stores.

As she walked across the parking lot, she saw a small cardboard sign in the shape of a man. It was a recent sales line for a reputable brand of oil. She didn't know why they chose that specific model because he was a little man who didn't look trustworthy or appealing. Something about the model reminded her of a weasel. At that moment, the damn thing made Salvia think of Jake. Before she knew it, Sal strode over to the sign and kicked what she imagined was Jake's stupid-looking face halfway across the parking lot.

She then considered going straight to Jake and confronting the lying bastard. However, when she looked at the condition of the sign she had just punched out, she thought it best to cool off first. Salvia went home, lay back into her new La-Z-Boy, and tried to push all these problems out of her mind.

Salvia made a sincere effort to concentrate her attention on women, except now, she felt that her self-presentation was tainted. She wanted to be able to tell a prospective partner that she had a decent job. This, to her, proved that she was hard-working and dependable and a good provider. But now that she was jobless, she could make no such claim. Despite her best efforts, Salvia Singleton joined the ranks of the unemployed.

✿✿✿✿

Friday, September 17

That Friday night, an early cold front blew in, bringing down the last of the autumn leaves that still clung stubbornly to the trees. Even the radio announcers complained that they were unprepared for the chill. But when Salvia returned to the gay bar that weekend, she at once felt warm and hopeful because she noticed new women, and they looked promising.

Two friendly women even danced with her briefly before quickly scurrying back to their friends. Although that was not exactly what Salvia wanted, she considered it a good start. Sal returned to her barstool and nursed her drink. She deliberately tried to make it last as long as possible because she didn't want to repeat her earlier mistake and dull her senses in any way. Besides, the beautiful women before her were enjoyable to watch, and while she was in the position of a voyeur, she wanted to savor such visions of loveliness.

Swiveling around on her stool, Sal hooked her brown leather boots on the rungs, leaned backward against the bar, and watched the women dance. These women looked like virtual goddesses with graceful curves, shining hair, and sensuous smiles. Sal noticed that most wore sensible shoes and little makeup, which she found even more appealing. To her way of thinking, they were down-to-earth, girl-next-door types. Only she knew that these young women were not the typical heterosexual girls next door, they were women who loved women, and this knowledge made them even more enticing.

Salvia watched their bodies swaying gracefully to the music. Her gaze drank in the outlines of the women in long-standing relationships, moving in swan-like unison until such pairs eventually melted together, pressing against each other in intimate familiarity. After consuming half a beer, a curly-headed brunette breezed in the front door. With surprise, Salvia realized that she recognized a person she had always wanted to get to know.

This realization made her incapable of nursing her drink. A sudden onslaught of thirst made Salvia gulp down her beer. The instant her drink ran dry, the bartender, a stocky young butch, was quickly at her service, providing a refill.

"Better move fast," the bartender whispered, "before she gets away."

Salvia arched an eyebrow, intrigued that the perceptive bartender thought her so obvious. But her encouragement helped. Salvia propelled herself off the barstool and glided toward the object of her desire.

"Hi," she said. "Do you remember me?"

Elena, her favorite sub maker, grinned. "Chicken salad sandwich?"

They both laughed. Elena was a lean and graceful-looking woman, barely an inch taller than Salvia. Soon, the two of them were dancing together, shy and tentative at first, but rapidly warming to each other.

Salvia was familiar with Elena's easy grin and cheerful voice, but she had not known the warmth of her body or the softness of her hands. Now slightly alcohol emboldened, Sal slowly moved in closer, then closer still, until they eventually came to dance with intimacy. Through song after song, she noted that for every small move she made, Elena reciprocated with similar movements, until the two women reached the point of gyrating and grinding their bodies together to the wild rhythm of the music.

Slowly, Salvia's feelings about her own behavior progressed from shyness and harsh judgment of herself—for performing a dance too intimate for public viewing—to a point where she no longer gave a damn. Her vision, senses, and emotions narrowed to a world where she and Elena were the only two people who existed.

Sal was enjoying herself immensely without thought of time or anything outside of the immediate sphere she was in. But unfortunately, as was common with life's finest moments, her time alone with Elena flew by too fast. The next thing she knew, the deejay was announcing the last dance. It was a declaration for which Salvia was ill prepared. Here the deejay was saying that the bar was about to close when she realized that she had learned little about this woman she desperately wanted to get to know. It dawned on her that in a matter of minutes, she might be watching helplessly as Elena slipped away.

Two conflicting emotions surfaced: every pore of her body screamed its desire to have sex with this lovely creature, a woman who was clearly giving this same message to her through intimate dance moves, but more importantly, Salvia wanted a relationship. Mentally, she wrestled on the course of action for her next move. She didn't know if she should ask Elena for her phone number or follow the physically suggestive lead she was given. The look on Elena's face soon told

Salvia that it was clear Elena wanted more.

"Would you like to come home with me?" Salvia mumbled into Elena's ear.

"What?" Elena asked over the loud music. But as she stood with her courage rapidly waning, Sal found that she was unable to repeat her impulsively intimate proposal. All she could do was stand impatiently and wait for words that would not come.

Just as she was pondering her next move, Elena leaned in and kissed Salvia passionately on the lips while caressing Salvia's butt with both hands. In this way, the decision was made for her.

Bravely, Salvia repeated her request. "Elena, would you like to come home with me?" "Where do you live?" Elena asked.

"West of here, on the edge of Golden," she said.

"Okay, I'll get in my car and follow you."

Salvia was overjoyed. She couldn't believe her good fortune. In her inexperience, she didn't know what she was doing, but somehow, she had managed to succeed anyway. She hadn't fixed up her house a minute too soon! Exiting the bar, they walked into frigid air and reluctantly parted for their cars. Chilly air made each outward breath visibly vaporous. It quickly enveloped the previously ardent women and viciously bit through Salvia's thin coat. It flowed like ice water across the surface of her warm body and seemed to penetrate even her thoughts.

Salvia quickly realized that frigid air had a sobering effect. What they were about to do might be normal behavior for gay men, but surely, it was impulsive and out-of-the-norm behavior for lesbians. Just as she reached her Jeep, Elena pulled up beside her in a green Honda. Sal grinned, and her heart leaped with joy. However, when she noticed a sheepish expression on Elena's face, her spirits plummeted.

"Uh, Salvia, it's later than I thought, and I…"

Graciously, Sal allowed Elena to back out. When she carefully guided her Jeep down the dark streets toward home, she felt very much alone. Salvia slammed her fist on the top of her dashboard.

"Damn!" she shouted. "Damn, damn, damn!"
***

Over the next few days, Salvia knew that her feelings toward women were slowly beginning to change. Born of sexual frustration and repeated rejections, her feelings evolved into a mixture of sensual desire and anger. Worst of all was that she was unable to suppress them. Lustful thoughts bubbled just beneath the surface, building pressure like molten lava, waiting for an opportunity for release.

Unbidden, sexual frustration moved to the forefront of Salvia's life. Everywhere she went, she thought about sex. In every sentence and every action, she discovered hidden sexual meanings and innuendo. Like a dieter unable to stop thinking about food, Salvia's lack of sexual opportunity caused her to similarly obsess about sex. To Salvia, it felt like a sex monkey had climbed onto her back, and it was hell bent to stay there.

Salvia also began to feel resentful toward young men. It was a mystery to her how un-groomed pimply-faced assholes could get women when she could not. To her amazement, young men attracted women even when they lied and made false promises. She noted that men were often successful despite their lack of limits as to how low they would stoop to achieve it. Worse yet, males often showed little regret for infecting their female partner with a sexually transmitted disease or for causing an unwanted pregnancy. Compared to them, she, Salvia Singleton, was undoubtedly the superior choice because she would never do such a thing to a woman.

Chapter Four: The Sex Monkey

Saturday, September 18

It was not fair! The playing field was not fair! On average, women earned twenty percent less than men earned. Therefore, Sal reasoned that it was easier for men to compete for women since they could afford to dress better and to own finer cars and houses. Salvia considered the belief of most women: that men did not earn more through superior skill or knowledge, but these higher salaries were handed to them on a platter because they had an ugly appendage hanging between their legs. Her job was a prime example; a less qualified male was given what Salvia had worked long and hard to earn. What a pile of horse shit!

One late afternoon, while guiding her Jeep onto the interstate, Salvia was thinking these thoughts when a young man in a red sports car sped up to keep her from merging into the ample space ahead of him. Knowing that he had seen her signal light and was deliberately trying to impede her, Sal continued to merge without a glance in his direction. She deliberately pretended not to see him, by facing forward and using the side mirrors to guide her Jeep into his lane. Of course, her actions frustrated him, and he blasted his horn for five full seconds. She smiled to herself and turned up the radio. He sped up, passed her, and gave her the finger. She laughed.

Ten minutes up the road, an even stranger thing

happened. Apparently frustrated with the slow progress of traffic, a small pickup truck tried to pass her illegally on the right shoulder. The truck didn't have mudflaps, and his tires viciously pelted her Jeep with dry bits of gravel. When their vehicles were dead even, Sal looked over and saw the face of yet another young man.

"What the fuck is the matter with you?" she yelled at her closed side window. Turning toward her windshield, she then yelled in a mixture of amazement and frustration, "Men think they own the whole damn world!"

Continuing illegally along the right shoulder, the truck sped up. But Salvia decided that this bastard was not going to cut her off, and he sure as hell was not going to pass her. She sped up accordingly. From fifty-five to sixty miles per hour, they drove, with both vehicles dead even on the highway. In the passenger seat of the white truck, which was ten feet from her, Salvia noticed a young woman appeared to be pleading with the driver. However, the driver ignored her and held his pace on the unstable shoulder. Both vehicles continued to accelerate. Her speedometer climbed from sixty to seventy miles per hour.

When Sal looked over, the passenger's face had turned red, and she was now shouting at her companion. Looking ahead, Salvia noticed a large metal sign firmly planted where the shoulder narrowed. If the idiot didn't slow down and drop behind her, his truck was destined to crash right into it. Sal smiled. I don't have to allow this ignorant jackass to pass me on the shoulder. Listen, buddy, you might be a young white male, but my Jeep is newer and a damned sight more powerful than your little truck! Then Salvia grinned wickedly. She had the power to box his dumb ass in, and she knew it.

As she gave her Jeep even more gas and pulled ever so slightly ahead of him, she mentally reviewed the situation. Since the moron really had no other choice at this point, she expected to see him drop back and drop back fast. But to her surprise, the young fool continued racing illegally on the shoulder. He was certainly not doing what any reasonable person would in his situation.

"You're even crazier than I am!" she muttered in disbelief.

The sign loomed closer. That big sign is sure gonna mess up your truck. It might even hurt. Suddenly, an adrenaline rush of sanity helped Salvia to stop thinking about the young male and to consider the well-being of his female companion. It's not your fault that he's an idiot, you just got stuck with him. Sal took one last look out the side window. The moron was keeping pace with her, and the sign was getting too damn close. Taking herself out of the race, Salvia veered left into the next lane and watched as the egomaniac beside her cut over just in time to miss the sign. As she slowed, the pickup truck took the lead, continuing its high rate of speed until it dropped out of sight.

Alone on the highway, Salvia looked out at the open fields of tall grass waving in the wind beside her and remembered a program on television about elephant societies. Elephants had little use for males in their herds. When they were cute babies, the matriarchal herd nurtured males. But once males became sexually mature, the females drove them away. Males were not allowed to return to a herd except for brief periods when needed for breeding purposes.

"Now they had the right idea!" she said aloud.

"Ah…to be surrounded by nothing but a society of women. Dang, I should've been an elephant!"

The Fire

Early Sunday, September 19

Salvia was having a bad dream. She had gone to Florida on vacation, but the weather was too hot to enjoy herself. The tropical climate was so humid that she was finding it difficult to breathe. She awoke from her dream with a start, shooting bolt upright in bed with the sudden realization that she was not on vacation, but at home in Colorado and that something was terribly wrong. It really was hot and difficult to breathe! Smoke was in her house!

The beige wall of her bedroom reflected orange from the living room. Sal threw back the covers and ran into the living room where, in near disbelief, she saw flames coming out of the back of her mother's old television set. Grabbing her new cordless phone, Sal ran back into her bedroom and dialed 911. The fire was still small but already producing smoke so thick that each inhalation became chokingly painful. Why didn't the damned smoke detector go off?

Her mind raced. Should she grab her valuables and run out of the house, or should she try to fight the fire? With firefighters on their way, she opted to fight the fire. Salvia ran to the laundry room, grabbed a dusty fire extinguisher, pulled the pin, squeezed the handle, and sprayed its contents over the flames. To her satisfaction, the chemicals of the extinguisher initially stunted the flames. However, as the fire died out, the smoke became thicker.

The old television set churned out gaseous emissions from its melted frame. The burning plastic was emitting an acrid gas that irritated her eyes and burned her lungs. She pulled her T-shirt over her mouth and continued spraying. By the time a fire truck arrived, she had nearly conquered the fire, but she was still happy to see them because they were experts who could take over while she went outside to breathe in fresh air.

Salvia staggered outside and coughed like she'd never coughed before. Bending at the waist, she experienced spasms so violent that she was certain she would puke. Falling to her knees on the grass, she watched as firefighters rushed into her house. Another firefighter unfolded a blanket and draped it over her shoulders. This caused Salvia to consider her appearance for the first time since she awoke. She was surely a pitiful sight as she was dressed in a T-shirt and nylon boxer shorts. Long strands of saliva were oozing from her mouth.

Salvia wiped her lips with the back of one hand as the tall firefighter, whom she now recognized was a woman, knelt beside her and offered her an oxygen mask.

"Is anyone else in the house?" the firefighter demanded.

"No," she said, emphatically shaking her head, since the oxygen mask covered her mouth.

"Any pets?" the formidable woman asked.

"No," Salvia again answered. "It's only me," she said as she envisioned a small family huddled together consoling one another. She was indeed all alone with no intimate partner to throw her arms around.

Sal spent the rest of the night in the hospital for treatment of smoke inhalation with her mind a whirlwind of thoughts. Six days ago, she didn't think it possible to wake up in the morning with her life in any worse condition. Obviously, she was wrong. Now she was jobless and homeless—at least temporarily. However, she did have two good things going for her: fire insurance and unemployment benefits. For the first time ever, she thought it just as well that she didn't have a job because she would need time off to clean up the post-fire mess.

Fortunately, Salvia's mother had selected a good insurance carrier, so that after the fire, the process of cleaning up progressed nicely. Owing to the smoke damage and smoke inhalation, the insurance adjustor insisted that Salvia temporarily move out. They offered to pay for lodging elsewhere, and Salvia accepted. However, rather than fork that money over to a motel, she decided she would save the money and move into her mother's makeshift vacation home in a desolate mountainous area of Colorado. The money would come in handy.

Her mother had named their second home the Baby Doe condo after Colorado's famous Silver Queen, a woman known as Baby Doe Tabor, who lived a life of rags to riches, then back to rags again. Around 1882, a wealthy man named Horace Tabor struck it rich with an extremely productive silver mine in the mountain town of Leadville, Colorado. He married a poor woman named Baby Doe, who became his second— and much younger—wife. The two lived a lavish life until the bottom dropped out of the silver market. Horace unsuccessfully tried to regain his wealth by gambling on other mines, but none of them panned out. After his death, Baby Doe wound up living in a supply shack and walking into town with rags on her feet. She eventually froze to death in that shabby place, and her own daughter refused to acknowledge her. The name Baby Doe came to stand for a poor person with visions of grandeur.

Since a true second home was beyond the financial means of Salvia's mother, she opted instead to buy an obscure piece of mountain land, then hired men to build a Quonset hut on it. The hut was a large steel storage shed in the shape of a giant half pipe. Inside it were basic comforts, because, according to county regulations, a hut was not a legal living space. If caught utilizing it that way, they could be fined and forced to use the building for storage only. However, her mother confidently stated they could pull it off. She told Salvia that their Baby Doe condo was a "poor person's vacation home," too isolated for trouble.

The gravel road that led to the building was narrow and seldom traveled. The hut itself was around a curve in the road and visible only for a moment, and even then, a person had to be carefully looking to spot it due to numerous large ponderosa pine trees.

The hut had a makeshift water system that consisted of a high hanging gravity-fed water barrel perched over their kitchen sink. It had a pot-bellied stove, kerosene lanterns, and a gasoline-powered generator that provided them with electricity and therefore lights and small electric heaters. However, its finest feature was the fact that it was built like Fort Knox. Its two windows could be covered by solid steel locking shutters. The one and only steel door was made doubly secure by a similarly huge pair of steel locking shutters. Their steel hut was virtually theft-proof and fireproof, two features that could be crucial in isolated Colorado mountainous areas.

After staying alone in it for two days, Salvia realized the place needed certain improvements and formulated ideas on how to complete such tasks. One of the changes Salvia wanted to make was to install a switch on two cheap wall-mounted lights. Currently, to turn them on, she had to fumble around in the dark with a plug in hand while trying to match up the prongs of the plug to the holes in the outlet. When plugging them in, a spark of electricity often made her wonder just how likely she was to get shocked. Salvia believed she could change the lights into fixtures that were far safer and more convenient by installing on/off switches. Since she was handy enough to make such a conversion and now had all the time in the world to do it, she purchased two switches and proceeded with her plan.

She removed the light fixtures from the wall and took them to the shed behind her fire-damaged house where she'd left her electric drill. The first thing she intended to do was drill a hole on the narrow side of one of the wall-mounted plates. She would then use that hole to install a pull chain switch.

With drill in hand, she got to work. Salvia was experienced enough with tools to know the safest way to drill a hole in metal, but she impatiently decided against doing so because the metal was so thin that she thought it unnecessary. The correct way was to tap a small indentation with a center punch or a dull nail. Such an indentation would serve the purpose of keeping a drill bit firmly on target. However, since the cheap gold-toned metal of the fixture was so thin that she could practically bend it with her fingers, Salvia assumed she had the strength to force the drill to bite into the metal by using pressure alone. This shortcut meant she would not have to bother finding a punch or nail.

Her quick and simple plan was to hold the light fixture in her left hand while she worked the battery-operated drill with her right. To her surprise, when she activated the drill, the spinning bit acted like a figure skater on ice; it danced and skidded across the surface of the fixture, instead of piercing it. Frustrated, Sal pulled back and lined the bit up again. Once the bit was back on its mark, she pushed the bit more firmly against the metal. This time, when the drill bit began spinning, it raced completely off the metal surface, and before she could yank her hand out of its way, its sharp tip bore a hole directly into the index finger of her left hand.

"Shit!" she yelled.

Salvia dropped the drill and looked at her finger in disbelief. A spiral of pink tissue had corkscrewed its way out of her finger and strangely, this corkscrew of flesh—her flesh—stood on end. For the briefest of moments, the small hole remained hollow and pink, but then, as if called belatedly into action, blood filled the hole and raced down her finger.

Holding her finger in the air, Salvia ran into the bathroom. Blood trickled down her left hand and down her arm. To avoid becoming a bloody mess, she tried lowering her injured hand, but that caused intense throbbing in her finger, so she raised her hand again.

Salvia yanked open the door to the bathroom closet and rummaged through the few items she had not discarded when cleaning the house. But try as she might, she was unable to find gauze. There were no gauze squares, no gauze rolls, and nothing sterile that looked absorbent. As blood dripped onto the tile floor, her search became almost frantic as she tore through the closet looking for anything that might do.

Eventually, she found a Kotex mini pad. She then ran into the utility room, and using her right hand and teeth, she managed to tear off a piece of duct tape and secure the pad onto her finger. Sal then wrapped her arm with a towel and headed for her Jeep.

The injury was deep enough that she knew she needed to go to the emergency room, but she didn't consider it dangerous enough to merit the expense of an ambulance ride.

Chapter Five: Robin Working in the Emergency Room

Saturday, September 25

With her RN badge in place, Robin hesitantly propelled herself down an unfamiliar hallway of the hospital. Had she known what she was walking into that evening, she would have called in sick! Neuro-trauma was where she liked working and fully expected to be stationed there that evening. She knew the patients on that floor and genuinely liked all her coworkers. However, when she arrived for duty, she was informed that the census on her floor was low and staffing too high. According to her charge nurse, she was needed in the emergency room. This was unusual because regular floor nurses could not perform triage. They must have been desperate. Robin accepted her assignment, but she did so reluctantly and with a heavy heart. When she reported to the ER nurse in charge, her reception was not a friendly one.

"Oh, great!" the doughboy-shaped charge nurse said sarcastically. "Whenever we're slow, we're always asking them to send down people so we can orient them to the ER, but of course, they don't do that. So now—and don't take this personally, cupcake—someone will have to orient you at a time when everyone is too busy to do it!" he snapped.

Robin shrugged. Even though she knew what he

meant, his rude comment made her feel like crap. She didn't want to work in the ER in the first place, and now this "queen" was insinuating that she was useless.

As an experienced and intelligent RN, she found his comments insulting. This grated on her nerves, but instead of walking off, Robin figured she could make herself useful by looking in on patients and monitoring and recording vital signs. However, Robin's duty crept along at a snail's pace. Feeling out of place, she repeatedly wondered how much longer it would be until dinner.

Robin wished that a coworker from her own floor had been sent along with her, someone she could talk to who might help make her shift go by a little faster. She figured, with a friend, she could have fun imitating the ungrateful doughboy who referred to her as "cupcake" and would allow Robin to turn her woes into a laughable situation.

Normally, when dinnertime rolled around, she ate with a coworker in a backroom on their own floor. However, nurses in neuro-trauma tended to snatch meals at the last minute, when and if they could even get them. It would be too difficult to coordinate dinner with a coworker. Then Bella came to mind. The first chance she got, Robin darted into an empty room, grabbed the phone, and invited Bella to join her. Being good-natured and flexible, Bella readily agreed. The plan was for her to come to the ER waiting room up front, and as soon as the charge nurse allowed her to do so, Robin would make a brief, but sanctioned escape.

After Robin called home, the Pillsbury-like charge nurse devised a new plan for Robin. He asked her to help the triage nurse in the reception area. Potentially problematic was that there was a certain amount of responsibility in ER admitting that placed a floor nurse like Robin in over her head. Nurses in the front were to prioritize ER patients since they could be in a life-or-death situation. But Robin figured if she was in doubt, she would ask a coworker. So she willingly went to the front of the emergency room because she knew this was where Bella would come to meet her for dinner.

Once there, Robin then systematically approached patients to ask routine admission questions, obtain their vital signs, and to fill out as much of the triage paperwork as she could. When Bella walked in, Robin grinned and asked her to wait a few minutes. She then called out a name and escorted a young man to the back. When she returned for her next patient, Robin stood for a moment, seeing a butch woman with a slightly bloody mini pad duct-taped over a finger on her left hand. This was not an unusual site for the emergency room; however, the fact that this stranger did not seem impatient or overly concerned that she was bleeding was abnormal.

When the staff wasn't bored, the emergency room was often a zoo full of panicked, impatient, and rude patients. Robin noted that instead of the injured woman watching the door leading to the ER, she was focusing her attention on one person: Bella! Even stranger still was that Bella seemed oblivious to this woman's attention. Instead, Bella appeared absorbed by an animal program on an overhead television set.

"Salvia Singleton," Robin called out.

"That's me," the injured woman said.

Reacting to the familiar sound of Robin's voice, Bella's gaze roamed from the television set to Robin and then to the woman with the injured finger.

"Well, good luck," Bella told her.

As soon as Salvia passed her, Bella grinned and winked at Robin. This was a look Robin knew well; it meant that Bella's gaydar was going off.

Chapter Six: The Birth of an Obsession

Saturday, September 25

As Salvia sat back on a narrow emergency room gurney surrounded by curtains, she mentally replayed her meeting with the dark-haired woman in the waiting room. Salvia had been awkwardly trying to open a can of Pepsi with her uninjured hand when this attractive woman came to her aid.

"Can I help you?' she had offered.

"Uh, sure," Sal managed to mutter. Noting her mocha brown skin, she decided the young woman looked like she was Hispanic. As Sal was wondering what it would feel like to touch such soft-looking skin, she had felt herself melting like butter to the kind woman's voice.

The stranger pried open her Pepsi and handed it back to Salvia with a polite smile.

"I don't know about you, but at a dollar a can, I sure would hate to spill it," Bella said.

As she smiled back at her, for a moment, Salvia forgot all about the throbbing in her finger. She wanted to interact with the woman, but unfortunately, her immediate attraction served to turn her into a complete idiot, silencing most speech with fear.

"Thanks," she finally muttered, while feeling her face flush with warmth.

Salvia became curious and wanted to ask the kind stranger what the reason was for her ER visit, but since the woman had no obvious injury or symptoms, she feared that asking such a question might prove too personal. The only thing Sal seemed capable of doing well was sitting quietly as she acknowledged her inexplicable attraction.

"What happened to you?" the woman asked Salvia.

"Oh, I, uh, um, I was trying to drill a hole in something and…I missed," Sal said.

"Oh, gee…that must've hurt!"

"No, it isn't too bad as long as I hold it up."

Salvia struggled to think of something intelligent to say, then suddenly blurted out, "But I just about puked when I saw the flesh of my finger all corkscrewed up in the air and then the blood came pouring out."

Bella grimaced, shuddered, and then said, "Ugh! I'll bet!" Then she moved away.

Salvia could have punched herself. What the hell is wrong with me? Why did I say something repulsive to someone I want to attract?

Feeling miserable, Sal stared unseeing at the freshly waxed floor. Despite her shyness, it was not long before she looked in the kind stranger's direction. Sal noticed that she had returned to the animal program on television and was no longer paying any attention to her. On one hand, it was disappointing she was not interested in Salvia, but on the other hand, her inattention left Sal free to study the woman without notice.

This woman was around twenty-eight years old. Her dark skin was a nice match for her bouncing black hair that had just a hint of curliness. She noticed the friendly woman was absently rubbing her hands together, reminding Salvia of a person who might be good at massage. Earlier, Sal had noticed the woman had soft brown eyes and a warm smile that caused two symmetrically perfect dimples to appear. Sensing that the woman was a lesbian, Salvia was happy to note that the woman was sitting alone.

But now, alone in one of the isolated back treatment areas, Salvia was undergoing a common process: treat, wait, treat, and then wait again. Robin, the nurse who led her back, had recorded her vital signs, then turned her over to another nurse, who removed the dressing and gently set clean gauze pads over her wound. Then that nurse left, and eventually, a doctor came in and numbed her finger. Then, to give the numbing medication time to work, he left. So again, she waited. Ten minutes later, the second nurse returned and thoroughly washed out her finger with a syringe full of normal saline. Watching fluid squirted in with so much force made Salvia grateful for the numbing medication. When the second nurse left, Salvia found herself alone again, waiting for the doctor to return. Either the doctor got very busy, or else it took considerable time for her finger to become numb enough for him to come back and stitch her up. Either way, Salvia was alone with her thoughts for a long time. In her mind, she continued to dwell on the attractive woman who had helped her open her can of Pepsi. There was no doubt in Salvia's mind that what she felt was a powerful attraction.

Finally, the doctor returned and stitched up her finger. Then, in the last step of Salvia's care, a male nurse came in and placed a unique sock over her finger, followed by a small metal brace. Salvia was given instructions about wound care and antibiotics and asked to sign her discharge paper. Quickly, she grabbed two prescriptions and rushed back to the waiting room to look for the woman. But she was gone. Half jogging out the door, Salvia reached the parking lot just in time to catch a glimpse of her as she drove away in a red Toyota with a rainbow sticker on the back window, and Salvia noticed the woman was still alone.

Without a rational thought, Sal jumped into her Jeep and followed her. When the woman reached her home, Salvia slowed her Jeep to take note of the number on her mailbox and the street sign at the end of the block. Knowledge of the woman's address felt important because, with such knowledge, Salvia now had the opportunity of a second chance. At this point in Sal's life—when she was feeling so powerless and out of control—now at least, she had an opportunity in hand to make future contact with the kind and attractive woman. Salvia held her bandaged finger at the top of the steering wheel and drove slowly up the mountain to the Quonset hut, comforted by this thought.

❧ ❧ ❧ ❧

For Salvia, each day of the next two weeks was dismal. The Quonset hut no longer felt like a vacation or an adventure. There was no television, and she had grown tired of reading. Salvia stopped being industrious. Her body felt drained of energy. Even the simplest of activities seemed to take a huge amount of effort. She also lost all desire to fix up the hut. At first, Salvia passed idle hours by sleeping. Then day, night, and time itself became of little consequence to her. Finally, even her sleep became erratic. She paced around the hut in the middle of the night. She lost her appetite and ate next to nothing.

She grew angry whenever she thought about her job and the guys she might never work with again. Then, with a pang of guilt, she came to realize that she even missed her mother. Salvia recognized that her life was spiraling into darkness; she had lost control and was slipping away, but she didn't know what to do about it.

In her clearer moments, Salvia recognized that frustration, anger, and depression were overwhelming her. Occasionally, she was even aware that she was perilously close to ending her pathetic existence. It saddened her to realize she was not getting better, only worse. It occurred to Salvia that her mind was taking charge by temporarily shutting down.

The only bright spot in Sal's dark thoughts revolved around the woman in the emergency room. Like candlelight dispelling darkness, she treasured the image of the kind woman's bright and dimpled smile. She longed to reach out and feel the softness of her skin. Salvia desperately wanted to make this woman her own. But she would first have to learn all about her. Currently, she didn't know the woman's name or even where she worked. Knowledge equals power. At that moment, Salvia vowed to learn more about this woman, much more!

Sal knew that stalking a woman was not right. But she found it simple to rationalize what she was doing. I'm not hurting anyone. In fact, no one even knows about it. And there was another plus, as well, because the activity of going out with a purpose made her feel a little better. At least she was doing something. Sal reasoned that she was acting out the role of a private detective.

     Author's name goes here

For the next week, Salvia secretly followed the woman of her desire. She slept little, and food remained unimportant, but at least she found a purpose in her life, and to that purpose, she dedicated herself completely. Eventually, her observations paid off. Sal learned that the woman's name was Isabella Sanchez, and she went by Bella. She learned that Bella worked part time for Jolly Rancher, a candy company in Golden, Colorado. Bella was also a freelance photographer and very fond of her wiry dog, which she often toted about in her car. Sal further learned that Bella visited a local coffeehouse on two afternoons of the week. "Wednesdays and Fridays, almost without fail," Sal said to herself as she sat alone in the parking lot at Starbucks.

One devastating piece of information blindsided her: Bella had a partner! How could I have been so stupid? Why did I think that someone as beautiful and kind as her was not already in a relationship?

Salvia learned that this dreaded partner worked as a nurse in the very hospital where she first laid eyes on Bella. But a partner didn't fit into her fantasy! In Salvia's mind, Bella was meant for her and her alone.

This last news made Salvia feel like someone had tugged at a final thread, starting an entire work to unravel. Sal had barely been keeping things together as it was. Losing her mother, losing her job, losing her house, being unable to meet women, living with terrible loneliness, and now, losing the one hope she had mercifully clung to was too much for her to deal with. She felt like she was drowning.

Salvia knew that meeting Bella, attracting her, and making the woman her own was one long shot of a fantasy to begin with. But once she learned that Bella had a partner, a woman who was a medical professional, Sal suddenly realized that her chance of winning Bella's heart was somewhere between slim to none. Frustration knocked her for a loop. Salvia was sick and tired of losing out. She wanted—no, needed—someone for herself. By God, she deserved it, too!

Salvia resolved that if she could not win Isabella Sanchez, then she would have to take her.

Chapter Seven: A Systematic Scheme

Midday Friday, October 8

One of the interesting things that Salvia learned while working at the auto parts store was that a vehicle identification number was stamped on a metal plate and attached to the dashboard on all vehicles. A VIN identified the vehicle and its registered owner. Further, these numbers were clearly visible from the outside of a car. While Bella was working at the candy company, Sal strolled past her red Toyota, looked through the windshield, and copied down the number. Then, she tried her hand at doctoring a car title and creating a fake ID. Finally, using her mother's makeup and large sunglasses, she dolled herself up, walked into the largest Toyota dealer in the area, and said she had lost her car keys. Sal handed the man her fake ID and doctored title, and then paid for a new key to Bella's car.

As she exited the dealer's parts shop with key in hand, Sal congratulated herself on her well-thought-out and smoothly executed plan. However, she was fully aware that taking possession of a simple key to someone's car was far less complex than taking possession of a real live human being. Salvia could not afford to underestimate the life-preserving moves of a captured person, and this, of course, would make an actual kidnapping far more difficult. She was very aware that people could be crafty devils, especially when they sensed they were in danger. She also knew that adrenaline could make a person extremely strong and unpredictable. Salvia resolved that whatever plan she devised had to involve either trust or the element of surprise. Given Bella's kindness, Salvia opted for trust.

❧ ❧ ❧ ❧

That afternoon, Salvia drove to Starbucks and waited for Bella to drive up, park her car, and go inside. A moment after Bella entered the building; Sal slipped the key into the door of the Toyota, released the hood latch, and disabled the coil pack, which was Toyota's newer version of a distributor cap. Then she closed the hood, locked the car, shoved her thin leather gloves into her pocket, and limped into the coffee shop. Once inside, she arranged her rainbow necklace so that it was clearly visible and began her preplanned act. In a credible performance, Sal limped across the tile flooring, favoring her left foot. She bought a cup of tea, then found Bella at a sunny table next to a window, slowly sipping on a latte.

"Hi...um...Don't I know you?" Sal asked.

Bella looked up. "Oh, yeah. We met at the hospital. How's your finger?"

"Oh, it's almost healed." Salvia held up her unbandaged finger, and then she hesitated hopefully.

Bella took the cue. "Are you alone? Would you like to join me?" "Yeah, sure...thanks." Salvia made a show of limping to the table.

"What happened to your foot?" Bella asked.

"Oh," Salvia said. "This must be my unlucky month. I accidentally stepped on a nail."

"Gee, I sure hope you have health insurance!"

"Yeah, I'm on workman's comp. I'm in construction," she lied. "What do you do?"

"I work in the human resources department at Jolly Rancher."

"You mean the candy factory?" Sal asked. "Do they give you free samples?" Bella smiled, producing those dimples Salvia found so attractive.

"No, they don't give us anything free, but they do give great employee discounts." "My name is Salvia," Sal said while reaching out to shake hands.

"I'm Isabel. But my friends call me Bella."

It was a warm handshake, but when she felt Bella pull back her hand a bit abruptly, she silently criticized herself for holding her hand a little too long. Damn, when it comes to women, I can't seem to do anything right. Then, trying to bridge this distance between them, Salvia quickly said, "My girlfriend's a nurse."

"Really?" Bella asked. "Mine is too! What's her name? Where does she work?"

Salvia's mind raced to produce a woman's name and a hospital on the other end of town.

"Debra McIntosh. She works at Aurora Central."

"Mine works at the hospital that you went to."

"Yeah?"

"Yeah, in fact, you met her! She was the one that called you back to see the doctor," Bella said.

"Oh, I didn't know that was your partner," Salvia said as she searched her memory. "Was she the tall one with brown hair?"

"Yeah, that one."

"I guess you already know that the only problem with being with a nurse is the weird hours they work," Sal said slowly. "Because it gets kind of lonely sometimes, you know?"

"Don't I know it?" Bella gushed.

Salvia tasted her hot tea, made a point of obviously scanning what was on the table, and then said, "Oh, dang!"

"What?" Bella asked.

"I forgot to get some honey for my tea, and now I'm gonna have to limp all the way back over there!"

"I'll get it for you," Bella volunteered. "How many would you like?" "Thanks. Thanks a lot. Two, please," Salvia said, grinning sheepishly.

Bella laughed.

It sure has been a long time since I've heard a woman laugh, and Bella's laughter sounds like cheerful music.

As Bella headed for the honey packets, Sal quickly fished an open sugar wrapper from her pocket that was filled with crushed pills—three of her mother's tranquilizers and one sleeping pill. Quickly, she reached across the table for Bella's coffee cup, poured the white powder into the frothy liquid, and stirred until it dissolved. Then she opened Bella's cellphone and dribbled a teaspoon of hot tea over the open charging port. Briefly, she allowed the tea to soak in, then dabbed the phone with a napkin until the surface was visibly dry and quickly pushed the phone back to its original position, just as she'd found it.

Bella returned with two packets of honey, and the two women chatted. Bella shared one of her and Robin's memorable camping mishaps while Salvia hung on every word, taking in Bella's frequent smiles and moments of laughter. Bella was delightful. She was so bright, funny, and trusting that a small pang of guilt crossed Sal's mind. But Salvia knew that if she gave up on her plan now, the nothingness that was taking over her life would grow into an unbearable monster.

When it came time to leave, Sal stalled by limping slowly toward her Jeep, carefully putting her gloves back on, and fiddling with her car keys. In contrast, she noted that Bella quickly unlocked her own car, appeared to put the key in the ignition and was visibly surprised when her Toyota didn't start. Frowning, Bella tried turning over her engine repeatedly until Salvia tapped on her window.

"What's wrong?" she asked.

"I don't know. It won't start."

"Pop the hood, and I'll take a look at it," Sal instructed.

Bella opened her hood latch, then got out to stood next to Salvia and watched while Sal pretended to examine the engine.

"I think maybe you have a crack in your coil pack," Sal said. "We can go pick up a new one if you like."

Bella frowned, sighed audibly, then put her hands on her hips. "No. I don't want to put you out. Besides, Robin can fix it for me. She might even be able to get a refund on the parts since she just did a tune-up for me."

"Okay, well, can I at least give you a ride home? I have the time, unless you're, like, forty miles away," Salvia said. But, of course, she knew exactly how far away Bella lived. Bella laughed. "No, I only live about five miles from here. I could practically walk." "Well, I couldn't," Sal said while looking down at her foot. They both laughed.

Once she had Bella safely in her Jeep, Salvia decided to stall for time by stopping for gas. Squeezing the handle of the gas pump ever so lightly, she pumped fuel into her Jeep as slow as was humanly possible. She then bought gum in the store, came out, and took a leisurely stroll around the side of the building to the bathroom. When she returned to her Jeep, she moved things around in the glove box, claiming the machine was out of receipt paper and that she needed a pencil and something to write on so she could record the amount of her gasoline purchase.

When they finally left the station, Bella said she felt powerfully sleepy and that she ought to call Robin and tell her about the problem with her car. Salvia involuntarily held her breath. But when Bella tried to use her cellphone, she had the same bad luck she had experienced with her car; it would not work.

"Dang, now my phone doesn't work!" Bella said. "It seems like everything's turning to crap today!"

Salvia merely looked at her, hoping she wouldn't make any connection between the two.

"Oh, well." Bella shrugged. "I'll call her when I get home. I'm really sleepy anyway. I must have a backward system because sometimes hot coffee in the afternoon makes me drowsy."

Traveling toward Bella's house, they were nearing their destination when Bella finally nodded off, allowing Sal to gently guide her Jeep in the opposite direction without her passenger taking notice. She steered the vehicle smoothly onto Interstate 70 West, then headed directly for her Baby Doe condo in the mountains.

The twenty-two-hundred-foot climb from Denver to Genesee Park along I-70 mechanically tested vehicles with the poorly maintained ones often failing to make it. But Salvia's Jeep, in tiptop condition, made the climb with relative ease as it approached the scenic

Genesee Bridge. As always, Salvia looked forward to the upcoming view. Evidently realizing a well-designed bridge at this location would nicely frame the mountain view, engineers did a bang-up job by cleverly framing it. When the climb leveled out, drivers were able to catch a breathtaking glimpse of a mountain range that made up part of the Continental Divide.

Just past the bridge was the Buffalo Herd Overlook. Sal scanned the area for sight of the great beasts. She had once seen a monstrous-sized fellow grazing so close to the sturdy fence that she had pulled over, walked right up to the fence, and snapped some great photos of him. But nine out of ten times, she didn't spot a single buffalo, and today was no exception.

During the journey, Sal often checked the speedometer and took pains to obey all rules of the road. With a drugged and kidnapped woman in her front seat, the last thing she wanted to do was attract the attention of the police.

She was grateful that she and Bella were both private people leading quiet lives. Had either of them been famous, an act of this sort might draw attention, but as things were, neither her movements nor Bella's absence were likely to attract interest, at least not before she had her captive safely tucked away.

However, despite her good fortune, Salvia noted that her hands were shaking as she tightly gripped the steering wheel. And her sense of achievement mingled with mild paranoia was causing her to check and recheck her rearview mirror and to feel like the criminal she had now become. She looked over at Bella, dozing innocently on the passenger side of her Jeep. Salvia realized not only that this was an attractive woman, but also an intelligent one with a will of her own, and

Sal reminded herself that she had to be careful.

When she wakes up, I'll bet she'll raise holy hell. Salvia vowed not to breathe a breath of relief until she had her captive safely locked away in her Fort Knox home.

Chapter Eight: Mission Accomplished

Early Friday evening, October 8

When at last they reached the final gravel driveway that wound along the untamed mountainside, Sal smiled, congratulating herself on having formulated a good plan and on executing it without a problem. Mentally, she reviewed the things that could have gone wrong but didn't. The medications might have failed to work, or Bella might have detected a strange taste and refused to drink enough of her tranquilizer-laced latte. Bella might have realized Sal had drugged her and called for help or tried to escape. Someone could have become suspicious and tried to stop them. But Salvia was lucky because nothing had gone wrong. Everything was just ticking smoothly along.

Salvia did not realize the full extent of Bella's sedation until it came time to get her human prize out of the Jeep. The drugged woman barely responded to her voice, and even that response was inconsistent. It also turned out to be a greater struggle to bring an unconscious person into the Quonset hut than Salvia imagined. First, she tried carrying Bella over her shoulder, but her limp body would not cooperate. Regardless of the hold Salvia tried to use, Bella's flaccid body kept slipping. Finally, she eased Bella from the Jeep to the ground, then pulled her into a semi-sitting position from behind.

Taking a quick moment to cautiously look around, Sal smiled at the solitude that was theirs. She brought her arms under Bella's and encircled her warm torso, pulling it toward her own. With her fingers laced together just below Bella's ample breasts, she dragged Bella's limp body backward. The heels of the smaller woman's feet skidded and bumped across the ground as her body slowly bridged the distance from the vehicle to the dark interior of the hut.

Done at last. Salvia had complete possession of Bella. The object of her obsession was right in the middle of her bed, nestled in the privacy of her small vacation house. Salvia was creating her own fairy tale.

Deciding not to fool with the power generator for the moment, Sal lit a lantern, sat on the edge of the bed, and stared at Bella for a long time. Like a small and tired child, Bella looked like she was in a relaxed and peaceful slumber. Lovingly, Salvia took a limp hand and sandwiched it between both of hers, then was surprised by Bella briefly grasping her hand in return. The movement was like the gentle and sweet grip of a child in their sleep. Yet to Sal, it became a warm and intimate connection, as if an empowering current of electricity raced through them both.

Using her other hand, she gently brushed Bella's dark hair away from her face. With an index finger, she searched for the place on Bella's cheeks where dimples appeared each time she smiled. At last, she no longer had to view Bella from a secretive distance, she could reach out and feel Bella's soft skin beneath her fingers.

"Isabella," she said softly. "Bella...my Bell." Salvia sat on the edge of the bed, looking down at Bella, and found herself wishing she could freeze this moment in time. Such a sweet woman who had grasped her hand for a split second. Yet Salvia was no fool. She recognized the moment as a wonderful opportunity but also one that would not last long. Bella would awaken, and when she did, she was liable to become frightened and angry. Salvia did not look forward to that. It was time to restrain her.

Sal considered that it might take months to develop a meaningful relationship with this woman. The two of them had crossed paths only twice, but in neither of those moments had any meaningful conversation taken place. There had barely been enough talk to inspire interest, certainly not enough time to plant the seeds of love and nurture it along.

The longer Salvia gazed upon her prize, the more turmoil she experienced. She didn't want to do something as forceful as tying up this trusting and gentle woman. She wanted more than anything for time to stand still, so she could continue to savor the ability to touch her soft skin.

Salvia stroked the warm skin of Bella's right arm and then imagined more tender skin in areas that were covered with clothing. This fabric was a barrier to her desire. Salvia knew she was already guilty of drugging and kidnapping. Certainly, both of those acts were wrong. She could hardly bear the thought of anything standing in the way of their closeness, not even Bella's shirt and pants. As if to justify her plan of action, Sal focused on two comforting facts: they were alone and not a soul would ever know whether she touched her or not, including Bella.

As her gaze roved Bella's body, she noticed that Bella's T-shirt was pulling hard against her neck. To her way of thinking, if Bella remained fully dressed, she would certainly not be as comfortable as Sal could make her. Salvia used comfort as the excuse she needed to peel off Bella's clothing. Sal used her strong arms to turn Bella's flaccid body, pushing and pulling until Bella was wearing nothing but her panties.

Taking Bella's white shirt in both hands, Salvia brought it to her face and inhaled deeply. She drank in the unique aroma of her body. It seemed miraculous that this woman, whom she had obsessed about from a distance, was here now, lying mostly naked before her, appearing so relaxed and heavily medicated that she would not suffer from feelings of self-consciousness. Bella was not aware enough to know that her clothing was gone or that she was being watched, and Salvia found this innocence alluring.

After a while, Sal left the bedside just long enough to start a fire in the pot-bellied stove. Then she returned to bed and sat beside her, fully clothed. Lifting and cradling Bella's head onto her lap, she leaned against the headboard and stroked Bella's shiny black hair.

Finally, she broke the silence as she talked in a calm and reassuring voice. Her words echoed slightly from the confines of the metal. "I admit I was taken in by you at first sight," Salvia said. "But over the past week, I've been learning who you are, what you like, where you go, and how you treat other people. What I'm saying, Bella, is that I know that you're an incredibly good and decent person. I wish things were different because if they were, I could tell you this to your face, but I can't do that. Not yet anyway. The way things are right now, you wouldn't understand. You see, I can't help that I fell in love with you."

Sal became tearful. Her heart yearned for someone to love her because that must be a wonderful heartfelt feeling—to have someone think about her often, wish her well, and try to please her. It was so fantastic that she could hardly imagine the idea of someone genuinely caring for and about her. It seemed to Sal that love would be a natural high. Her body warmed to the idea of a woman seeing her for who she truly was and wanting her!

Briefly, her throat tightened, and she could not go on. But at last, she pulled herself together.

"I, uh, don't have very much to offer you. I'm not rich or anything. But since my mother died, I do have a house that's paid off. I also own this metal cracker box of a vacation home. I have a Jeep, too, and it's nearly paid for." Salvia sighed deeply. "I know it looks bad that I don't have a job, but I'll get another one. Then when I have work again, I'll show you that I can be steady and dependable. I'm handy, too. I can fix things. I mean, uh, well, gee, this is harder to say than I thought it would be. Um, I guess what I'm trying to say is that I feel like I've spent years and years building up this increasing supply of love. At the time, it didn't make any sense, but now, with you in my arms, it feels like pieces of a puzzle have magically fallen into place. Like all this time, I was waiting for the right person to come along," Sal said. Gently, she brushed the side of Bella's face with one hand.

"Bella," Sal said to the sleeping beauty in her lap, "I will share everything I own with you, and I will treat you right. I will do everything that a mate promises in marriage. I will love, honor, and protect you. I only want to keep you safe."

Then, lowering her own body beside her naked captive, Salvia petted and spooned with the unconscious woman. She discovered that Bella's flesh was pleasingly soft and tantalizingly warm beneath her touch.

However, in Sal's mind, it was problematic that Bella had already paired up with a nurse. There was no getting around the fact that this was bound to complicate things. No one could predict whether Bella would ever forget her partner. And although she envisioned Bella eventually becoming receptive to her, Salvia was realistic enough to recognize that all of this might take an extraordinarily long time.

"I wish there was a way to make her love me," she muttered toward the arched metal ceiling.

It was then that Salvia first considered brainwashing. It was an idea that revolved around certain words said to a person, what that person heard—even in a state of altered consciousness—and the necessity of them hearing it multiple times. Sal knew that brainwashing was a technique requiring patience and time, and now that she had Bella tucked safely away in her hut, she decided that she was rich with patience and had unlimited time. Salvia decided that this was how she would convince this kind woman to love her: She would plant the idea in Bella's mind that she and Salvia were lovers.

Sal wove a tale of the lives they had shared together by providing false details. Calmly, she voiced these imaginary details, then repeated the same information over and over again. Desperately, she wanted such ideas to become attached and remembered as real. Combining soft touch with repeated phrases, Sal started to believe that it was possible for Bella to react positively to her, even if only on a subconscious level.

"I am Salvia. Salvia is your lover," she chanted softly. "I love you. You love me. We are together. We were meant to be together. Isabella and Salvia. Bella and Salvia. Bella Mae and Salvia Lou. Bell and Sal. We are a couple." Softly, she chanted such phrases, repeating her words in a monotonous voice that somehow felt comforting. Through the rest of the night, Salvia committed herself to this task. She chanted and caressed Bella's gentle face and soft hands while trying to reprogram her subconscious mind.

Salvia traced the outline of Bella's smooth shoulders with an index finger. She felt the graceful curve of her waistline with the palm of her hand, and she gently patted the skin of her curvaceous buns. She cooed and petted Bella until Sal realized that she herself had begun to ache with desire. It was at that moment that she pulled away. She withdrew because she knew they were missing an essential element of a relationship: reciprocating desire. Although Sal believed she might eventually tease desire out of Bella, she decided that she would never force it. Starved of intimacy, Salvia had to restrain her impulse to lie next to Bella. It's wrong to take advantage of a woman's state of unconsciousness, to touch her without her permission or presence of mind.

Her sense of honor kept her from further contact.

Moving to her side of the bed, Salvia shook her head sadly as she thought about her own life. How is it that a person can spend an entire lifetime in such terrible loneliness?

By morning, Bella began to stir a little. Taking acute notice of all such movements, Sal felt a pinprick of fear. She didn't wish to lose control of this situation, not even for a minute. If things went wrong, this could indeed happen quickly.

Tenderly, Sal brushed Bella's cheek. "Eventually,

you will come to love me," she said. Then she slowly rose, kissed Bella gently on the forehead, and turned away. Crossing the room, she fetched four padded leather restraints.

Chapter Nine: She's Gone!

Late Friday, October 8

Robin got off work on time for a change at exactly eleven fifteen p.m., which was uncommon for a conscientious nurse, due to all the details patients often tended to pop up with whenever their nurse tried to leave. By eleven thirty, Robin was already approaching their house. As she eased into the driveway, she noticed the absence of Bella's car. While this was unusual, she didn't find it alarming. Bella may have impulsively taken off to the all-night grocery to pick something up. Since it was Friday night, there was the remote possibility that she'd gone to the bar with friends. That seemed unlikely because Bella didn't care for going to bars without her.

When Robin opened the garage door into the house, she noticed no lights were on inside. This would have made her fearful of a break-in except Rusty was there to greet her with her usual wild enthusiasm. She patted Rusty on the head and checked the house for Bella, but there was no sign of her. There was no note, no message on the answering machine, nothing.

Disappointed, Robin felt a brief pang of self-pity. She was not in the mood to be alone.

She went ahead with her usual routine, which was to change clothes, take a quick shower, put on her cotton pajamas, and fix herself a light snack. This was the time of night when she liked to unwind by talking to Bella or zone out in front of the television. She didn't have to bother with taking the dog outside because their pampered pooch had her own dog door. Rusty begged for food, so Robin jerked open the refrigerator door and looked for the half-open can of dog food she had stored after she fed the dog at breakfast. If the can was gone, it meant Bella had fed Rusty her dinner, as usual but it was half full and remained exactly where Robin had placed it. Now she was getting angry. Just how long has Bella been gone, anyway?

Robin mixed wet and dry dog food for Rusty and then dialed Bella's work just in case she was covering a last-minute night shift position. She recalled that Bella had not answered when Robin called her during a break at work, but that wasn't unusual. But now it was late.

Trying to remain logical, Robin decided the best thing to do was to call Bella's sister. If Bella had called Bonita, she might know where she had gone. Bonita said she hadn't heard from her, and she had no idea where Bella might be.

❧ ❧ ❧ ❧

Robin piloted her vehicle first to their all-night grocery store and then to the bar. When she was unable to find Bella at either place, she muttered aloud, "So help me God, Bella, I ought to wring your neck!" But even as she said this, uneasiness crept into the pit of her stomach.

When Robin came home to an empty house for the second time that night, she was truly worried. Still, she tried to remain logical. If Bella had been in an accident, it might not have been possible for her to call home. Robin started calling various emergency rooms.

When the ER idea didn't pan out, she decided it was time to ask for help. Noting her hands were shaking, she called her best friend, Marie. Robin had known Marie for six years and her partner, Squeaky, for three. Even though it was the wee hours of the morning, they were the kind of friends Robin could count on, and they rushed right over. The three of them sat in the kitchen and brainstormed.

Marie, a thick-waisted capable butch and great softball coach, thought it was time to call the police. But Squeaky, her skinny blond partner, felt that they should make more phone calls first. In her typical high-pitched voice, Squeaky reasoned that the gay community was a tight knit one and were best equipped to find one of their own. So, they called everyone they could think of, waking people up, asking questions, and being disappointed until at last, Squeaky gave up and agreed with Marie. The two of them encouraged Robin to call the police.

Unfortunately, the police said they would not declare an adult missing until they were gone for at least twenty-four hours.

"I'm going to call my cousin Sandy," Marie suddenly announced.

"That's a great idea," Squeaky said. She turned to Robin. "She's a detective in this area. Also, she's one of us. Sandy will help us; I know she will."

Chapter Ten: A Terrible Awakening

Saturday morning, October 9

Early morning sunlight flooded through the east window of the Quonset hut in an oblong patch with a shadowy crossbar transecting the center. The beam of sunlight crossed the room in stealthy silence, warming the floor, and then slowly climbed up the side of the bed until it fell across Bella. The light crept up Bella's lightly covered body. It illuminated her shiny hair and highlighted her smooth unblemished complexion.

Bella felt extremely drowsy, and she struggled to awaken because something did not feel right. She couldn't move freely, and her eyelids felt heavy. When she forced her eyes open, her vision was blurry. She blinked in the vain hope that this would improve her situation. When her vision did not clear, she laid her head back and tried to recall what could have caused her body to react like this. She felt unusually tired and unable to recall the events of last night.

This feels like ae hangover from hell. Strangely, though, she didn't remember alcohol being a part of her evening. Bella hardly ever touched hard liquor, and she didn't like beer. It wouldn't have been like her to go and get drunk. Why then, couldn't she remember where she was last night? Why could she barely pry her eyes open, and why was her vision so blurry?

"What is wrong with me? I need to get up," she

mumbled to herself.

She tried to move but couldn't. Her lethargic body was weak and uncooperative. It slowly dawned on her that it was not only her body that restricted her movement. Something was holding her wrists.

Again, Bella opened her eyes and tried to make sense of the blurry scene before her. When she looked down at her hands, she realized that both wrists were shackled with leather restraints like those Robin had described were sometimes used on confused patients at the hospital.

However, Bella had never been confused and certainly was not crazy, so unless she had experienced an accident that caused a brain injury, there was no justifiable reason for anyone to tie her up. Bella jerked her arms toward her stomach, but they barely moved before the leather straps attached to the restraints grew taut. The restraints held firm.

Similarly, she tried to jerk her knees up and discovered that her ankles were also bound. When the light cover slipped aside, she looked in disbelief at the uncovered flesh of her own body and realized that she was nearly naked. *Jesus, I'm half naked and completely immobilized! It's just like Robin to do something crazy like this!*

That idea didn't make sense. If it were Robin, then she would be at home, and this…was not home! Above her was a gray arched ceiling, and even though she couldn't see it clearly, she knew it wasn't familiar.

"What is going on?" she muttered in confusion. *Is this a hospital? Did I fall and hit my head? Did nurses have to tie me down because I was confused? What kind of hospital looks like this?*

"Nurse?" she called tentatively.

No one answered.

Bella lay still and focused on the sounds in the room. Except for gentle crackling noises, it was unusually quiet; an extreme stillness existed with which she was unfamiliar. She heard no voices in the background and no distant hum of traffic as was common when cars moved up and down the narrow street in front of her house. She couldn't even hear the distant sounds of dogs barking or children playing. An eerie stillness was all that existed.

She turned her head. This was not her bed, and it was not her house, of this much she was certain.

"Nurse!" she shouted.

But no one answered. The fact that she was not in a hospital room became a certainty.

Did I crash at a friend's house last night? But surely no friend I know would tie me down. Nothing made sense to her uncharacteristically lethargic mind. The confusion and diminished faculties caused her to feel increasingly vulnerable. Where in the world was Robin?

"Robin?" Bella called softly.

There was no answer.

"Robin!" she called as loud as her dry throat allowed her. Her tongue felt heavy. She realized she was very thirsty. The room remained quiet except for crackling noises. She sniffed the air, smelled the aroma of a fire, and noticed that she was uncomfortably warm. Bella repeatedly blinked her eyes and shook her head, trying to gain control of her sight and rid herself of mental cobwebs. If I can just get my head straight, there may be a rational explanation for all of this. Did someone drug me? Am I in a loony bin or someplace worse? Have I been raped?

Bella tightened her vaginal and anal muscles, trying to figure out if she felt sore down there. To her relief, she did not. Then she lowered her head back onto the bed and closed her eyes.

As she did so, a creepy thought entered her mind. Someone might be waiting for me to wake up! If something is about to happen, please, God, let my head be clear!

Bella never liked the effects of drugs. The notion of taking in anything that might diminish her mental ability had always felt unappealing. She didn't understand people who wanted to dull their senses. Whatever was going on with her, she would rather experience it fully. Even now, if something horrible was about to happen, she would rather have a clear mind. At least that way, there was always a chance, however slim, that she could talk her way out of it.

Suddenly, Bella heard someone approaching the outside of the building. There were sounds of rustling leaves and a rhythmic crunching that sounded like heavy boots walking on gravel, noises that became clearer as someone approached. As the crunching became louder, she grew tense with anticipation.

Bella unclenched her fists and twisted in her restraints, but they held firm. There was a brief silence and then the sound of someone stomping their feet, as though they were knocking off bits of gravel or ice that clung to the soles of their boots.

A lock clicked, and she heard creaking and groaning as a large metal door was rolled open. A gust of frigid air shot through the previously warm room. The wintry blast stunned Bella but also helped to revive her. Her mind felt more alert, even though her vision remained impaired. Then the heavy door groaned on its way closed, and the flow of chilly air ceased.

"Robin?" Bella asked in a frightened whisper.

No one answered.

"Robin, this shit is not funny," she said, clinging to a tiny shred of hope. But in her heart, she knew that Robin would never take a joke this far. Sensing movement in the room, she followed the sound with her head. Her eyes discerned only the silhouette of a person but no discernable features.

Bella stared at the foot of the bed where she hoped to see the long and lanky image of her partner. What she saw instead was an outline of a shorter person, thicker in girth, and that person was clearly not Robin!

"Oh, my God." She gasped. Her drug-addled mind struggled to recall the last place she had been. Salvia's Jeep. She remembered trying to go home and then the inside of the Jeep as the place where she had gotten drowsy.

Bella lowered her head back onto the bed, closed her eyes, and briefly gave in to the drowsiness.

❧❧❧❧

Bella awoke later and lifted her head again. "Hello?" she whispered uncertainly. "Is anyone here?" She noted that brighter sunlight was streaming through a window, and a blue jay was squawking in the distance. She waited for an ungodly amount of time, hoping as she waited that her vision would improve.

Periodically, she shook her head lightly and blinked hard, trying to clear her sight. As time crept along, the gravity of her situation sank in. Her survival was at stake. Lovingly, she thought about all those dear to her—Robin, her sister, her young nephews, and

Rusty. She had brief recollections of her last birthday, and now she wondered if today was as long as God was going to allow her to live. Bella reflected on her life. It had been a good one but a life that she had previously envisioned with a long future stretching out before her, a future, she now realized, that may not exist.

❧ ❧ ❧ ❧

Bella must have dozed off again because the next thing she knew, someone was gently brushing the palm of their hand across the side of her forehead. Bella's eyes flew open, and she raised her head. Again, she tried to bring her arms in and was instantly reminded that she could not do so.

Only this time, she clearly saw the person beside her.

"You? What are you doing here?" Bella asked.

"Taking care of you," Salvia answered.

"Where am I?" she demanded.

"An abandoned Air Force Base," Salvia lied.

Bella's gaze roved over the strange metal building, and she believed her. "Why? What happened to me?"

"Nothing."

"That's not true," Bella said. "Someone drugged me. Who would do a thing like that?" "It'll wear off," Salvia said.

Suspiciously, Bella looked around, but she saw no one other than Salvia. "Who else is here?"

"No one."

"No...one...else...is...here," Bella slowly repeated.

"No," Sal said, "there's no one here but me."

"Then how did I get here?"

"I carried you."

"Where are my clothes?"

"Over there."

"Why am I tied up?"

"Because" Sal said patiently, "you might try to escape."

With that, Bella unsuccessfully tried to sit up. "You're damned right I'd try to escape!

This is kidnapping! You don't have any right to do this to me!"

"I wonder," Salvia said pensively. "When it's a full-grown adult that's abducted, why do they call it kidnapping?" Salvia smiled and continued with her twisted logic. "I'm not a kidnapper," she said. "I'm a woman-napper. I took a woman." Then she chuckled at her own joke.

"What the hell are you going to do with me, hold me for ransom?" Bella asked.

"Nah," Salvia said as she scooted forward. "I'm not interested in money, and besides, trying to get some kind of ransom would be a great way to get caught. But I don't plan on getting caught. That's how kidnappers get caught, you know, when they try to squeeze ransom money out of someone," Salvia said.

Bella found this thought strangely disturbing. Robin doesn't know where I went, and since this nut doesn't want money, she won't be calling Robin, not for any reason.

"What are you gonna do, cut me up?" she yelled.

However, the moment Bella blurted this out, she pictured old headlines about a man-eating creep named Jeffrey Dahmer, which made her suddenly wish she had kept her mouth shut. She also thought about the finger injury that this strange woman had experienced, the so-called "accident" that brought her to the emergency room. In retrospect, she wondered if it had truly been an accident.

"I'm not going to hurt you," Sal said.

Bella didn't believe her, but she said nothing. I trusted this woman once, and this is where it got me! Not smart to hop in the car of a stranger!

Then, Bella made the conscious decision to yell at the top of her lungs, "Help! Someone help me!"

Salvia calmly sat on the edge of the bed and watched her. "No one can hear you. There's nobody here but me."

Again, Bella didn't believe her. It occurred to Bella that Salvia was trying to calm her down so she would stop yelling because she was afraid that if Bella yelled loud enough, someone in the area might hear her. Few places around Denver or Aurora were so remote that there was no one in the area. So she screamed at the top of her lungs. She threw her head back and yelled for all she was worth. Bella screamed like a woman in a horror movie.

Responding to all the noise, Sal got off the bed and paced about the dimly lit Quonset hut. Bella noticed that Salvia had a strong and steady gait without any hint of a limp. As she watched her pacing, she also noted that she was a powerfully built woman. Salvia's hair was a little disheveled, which made Bella wonder if these were warning signs of insanity, signs that she had somehow missed during their encounter in the coffeehouse. This fear fueled her desire to keep yelling. Bella screamed until her throat grew tender. She yelled until Salvia finally gave up and went outside. As Salvia was leaving, Bella tried to take advantage of the situation during the brief period when the door was open, by screaming especially loud. Surely, there was a possibility that someone would hear her. Someone might happen to come along. But no one came to Bella's rescue.

When the door closed, Bella again tried to slip out of her restraints by pointing her fingers and bunching them together like a cable, which made her narrow hands even narrower. She pulled until the skin on the back of her hands ached and the muscles in her shoulders felt sore. But it was no use. They were high-quality restraints that were fastened securely. She was not about to escape. By the time Salvia finally came back inside, Bella was almost eager to see her.

"I told you that no one can hear you," Sal calmly repeated.

In her mind, Bella considered the vast desolation of an abandoned Air Force Base. If Salvia believed that someone might be around and hear her screams, then all her yelling would have alarmed the woman, but that hadn't happened. Although she appeared slightly irritated by her screaming, it obviously was not alarming. Not once had Salvia gone to a window or door to peer outside.

As it was, Bella's screaming may have merely served to give this unstable woman a headache. Bella took a deep breath and then a long and resigned exhalation. It's time to face the truth. I made a mistake by allowing myself to trust this woman that I thought was harmless. Salvia is crazy, she has to be. For heaven's sake, she drugged and kidnapped me! When she did that, she showed no respect for my safety or my personal freedom. Now I'm helplessly bound to a bed, for God only knows what reason, and with nothing useful at my disposal...unless I can use thoughts and words to my advantage. The only trouble is, logic and reasoning might be useless on a woman who has lost her mind.

"Please," Bella said in a near whisper. "Please let me go! I won't tell anybody. Nothing will happen to you. We can both just pretend that this never happened."

Sal leaned forward. "But it did happen."

"But it's not too late to change a mistake like this."

"Who said it's a mistake?" Sal asked.

"You can't just grab someone off the street!" Bella said.

"But I did."

Suddenly, Bella wondered if this woman had kidnapped anyone else. "How many times have you done this?"

"You're the first."

"Why me?"

"Because I like you. I liked you the first time I laid eyes on you."

"You like me?" Bella repeated. "You like me?" she said in a raised voice of disbelief. "God Almighty, if you like someone, you're supposed to flirt with them, court them, and allow them free will. Haven't you ever heard of ladies' choice?" "I couldn't have won you," Sal said quietly.

Sensing the truth in her words, Bella made no attempt to answer. "Well…someone else then!" she snapped.

"I didn't want anyone else."

"What are you going to do with me?" "Keep you for my own."

"Keep me? You mean, like, forever?"

"Yeah, like, until death do us part."

"Jesus! You are a nutcase! I didn't marry you."

But her words were cut short when Salvia leaped

to her feet and shouted menacingly,

"Don't you ever call me a nutcase! Do you hear me?"

But Bella couldn't respond because Salvia had grabbed a small pillow and shoved it hard against her mouth. Bella tried to turn her head to the side for better breathing to no avail.

Salvia's voice was one of pure rage. Bella felt tiny droplets of spittle hit her forehead just above the pillow as Salvia yelled at her from close range.

In her restraints, Bella tried to bring an arm up in defense but couldn't. She tried to breathe but couldn't. She tried to kick by bringing up her knees, but the restraints held fast.

Being restrained and unable to breathe was the most frightening experience of her life!

"Ahh!" she cried while fighting her shackles and trying to jerk her head from side to side. But it was no use. Salvia was too strong. Salvia continued to hold the pillow so tight over Bella's mouth that Bella could not catch a breath. Bella began to feel hot and weak, and then, she was no longer able to struggle.

I'm going to die. However, just when that thought popped into her mind, Salvia removed the pillow.

Wide-eyed, Bella gulped for air. She now feared the unpredictable woman even more.

Bella gasped for air as her mind struggled to help her survive. She felt the adrenaline rush of clarity. She sure as hell is a nutcase, but I better never call her that again!

"I'm sorry," Bella sputtered as soon as she was able to speak. "I didn't mean to call you names."

"Are you okay?" Sal responded.

"Yeah, I'm all right."

Salvia gently stroked the side of Bella's arm. Bella remained still and allowed it. It was time for a different tactic.

A long and uncomfortable silence ensued as the two women recovered from their ordeal.

Salvia hung her head. Bella slowed her rapid breathing and tried to collect her thoughts.

"Salvia, I'm thirsty," she finally said. "All that screaming has just about made me lose my voice."

Sal grinned at the unexpected confession. "I'm not surprised."

Salvia fetched a bottle of water from a small cooler and lifted Bella's head from the pillow with one hand at the back of her neck to allow Bella's lips to meet the cold rim of the bottle. As the cool water eased down her throat, the dryness ceased. When the bottle was empty, Salvia lowered her head back to the bed.

"Thank you," Bella said.

"You're welcome."

"Look, I'll do whatever you want, but please just don't do that again, okay?" Bella hoped for a response but didn't get one. The metal building remained unnervingly quiet.

Since Sal didn't answer her, silence may have been the safest course of action, but Bella's mind couldn't be still, and she couldn't stand the silence. "Salvia…is that your real name?"

"Yeah."

"Is that what you would like me to call you?"

"Yeah."

"Okay," Bella said, and then her mind suddenly went blank, and she could think of nothing else to say. The two women sat in silence until Salvia eventually fetched a book and began reading to Bella.

Chapter Eleven: The Search Begins

Saturday morning, October 9

Sandy picked up the phone on the second ring, throwing her muscular legs over the edge of the bed and clearing her throat. A call for help from her cousin Marie was unexpected and alarming. Marie said a friend was missing, and no one knew where she had gone. Sandy felt this one in her gut. Marie and her friend were lesbians. This meant that the missing woman was one of her own. And naturally, when the missing person was a woman, Sandy experienced the same fearful thoughts of sexual violence that all women feared—even detectives.

Undoubtedly, the biggest difference between Marie and Sandy was that Marie felt certain that foul play was involved, while Sandy's mind remained open to all possibilities. Police officers were suspicious by nature, and Sandy was no exception. Experience taught her that this disappearance could be anything from murder, kidnapping, or rape to something as simple as a woman involved in a secret love affair. It was too early to jump to conclusions.

Having left her police SUV in her driveway, Sandy hopped into her personal car, a black 2002 Mazda Miata, shifted it into gear, and heard the deep-throated engine purr. The car was a present from her partner, Birdie, along with the police radio mounted under the dash. Sandy thought the presents were nice but unnecessary as she was not really a material girl. Just before the presentation of the car, she had been looking at a used Subaru Forester and would even have been quite happy with a pickup truck. She understood that giving presents was important to Birdie, so she graciously accepted and pretended to adore all the gifts Birdie gave her. On nice days, she often lowered the Miata's vinyl top and enjoyed the feel of wind on her face. But unfortunately, the car was so dangerously low to the ground and painted such a dark color that she worried that other drivers failed to see her.

Sandy bit her lip, briefly thinking about Birdie, a woman who tried to make up for what she could not seem to give her.

When she reached the address that Marie had provided, Sandy strode up in khaki pants and a navy-blue police polo shirt that outlined her muscular body in ways that the lesbians gathered outside could not help but notice. A handful of women stopped talking mid-sentence. Since she had spent her life feeling too tall and too big, as usual, Sandy didn't notice that she was considered attractive to lesbians. Owing to her substantial height and broad shoulders, ninety percent of women's blouses didn't fit her. Most women's clothing made her feel like some kind of freak. Being so tall, particularly in her adolescent years, had caused her to experience moments of great physical awkwardness.

Once her physical strength and natural athleticism began to serve her well, Sandy thought of her strength principally in terms of self-defense. She knew that most men, at least the smaller ones, were not particularly attracted to her. As for women, Sandy thought Marie was kidding when she told her that other lesbians thought she resembled an Amazon warrior. Her sandy blond hair and green eyes were a little unusual for someone of French descent, but her difficult-to-pronounce last name was very French in origin.

Marie stepped forward, met Sandy, and then stepped back, allowing Sandy to take over.

"Okay, ladies, listen up!" Sandy began, sounding like their softball coach. "My name is Detective LePersiller. I was called here by my cousin Marie. Since no one in my department can pronounce my last name, they call me Lady Persevere." She paused while the women chuckled.

Unbeknownst to all except Marie, it was a nickname that suited her well because Sandy was known for her determination to continue working cases even after a trail had gone cold.

"First of all, this is not an official investigation. I'm here on my own time and because I want to help my cousin and our community," she said. "It's a pity that so many adults are so irresponsible that they frequently disappear because that kind of careless behavior is the reason police departments have had to formulate the twenty-four-hour rule."

Sandy looked around at about two dozen women's faces and wondered if she had made the point that they should not blame the police for forcing distraught families to wait twenty-four hours before allowing a person to be declared missing.

"It's especially unfortunate for a person like Bella who is responsible," Sandy continued, "because there's a narrow window of time after a person goes missing before clues are lost forever. That's the other reason I'm here. We should jump on this right away. So this is what I'm going to do. First, I'm going to question

Robin, then I'm going to formulate a plan. Once we have a plan in place, I'll come back and ask you all for specific help. So hang tight, okay?"

She noted the attentive faces of the women and two men on the outskirts of the crowd.

They nodded in agreement.

Marie guided Sandy and Robin through the empty living room and into the kitchen where both women remained standing.

"Robin," Sandy said gently, "I'm sorry to hear about Bella's disappearance."

"Thanks."

"So far, from what Marie has told me, it sounds like you've been doing the right things.

But I need to ask some questions, okay?" "Sure."

Sandy gave Marie a look, and Marie left the two women alone.

"Okay, Robin, do you and Bella live here together?" Sandy asked.

"Yes."

"How long have you been a couple?"

"Seven years."

"Have you had any recent arguments?"

"No."

"None?"

"None."

"Has Bella ever disappeared before?"

"No, never."

"Does she have family in the area?"

"Yes, she has a sister, but I've already called her. She said she has no idea where Bella might be, but she's on her way over here."

"Has Bella been depressed lately?"

"No."

"Does she have any medical issues, such as heart problems, seizure activity, or diabetes?" "No."

"Do you think it's possible she might have gone to a bar?"

"No."

"Why is that?" Sandy asked.

"Because the only bar we ever go to is The Side Door. Everybody knows each other there, and the friends we've called said they haven't seen her."

"What about the other gay bars in town, have you checked those?"

"No, but I don't even think she knows where the others are located," Robin said.

Sandy smiled to herself. If an affair was in the making, women had a way of discovering previously unexplored bars.

"Does she have any usual places where she eats lunch, or does she frequent any coffeehouses?"

"Yes, she likes to go to Starbucks, the one on that big intersection down that way," Robin said.

"Marie told me Bella's car is missing," Sandy said. "What kind of car is it, and do you have the license plate number?"

"It's a red 2003 Toyota Corolla. I wrote the license plate number on this paper."

"Is there any damage to the vehicle or any bumper stickers that might make it stand out?"

"No, there's no damage, but there is a rainbow sticker in the back window."

"Okay, good. Now have you called any hospital emergency rooms?"

"Yes. But they didn't have her."

"What about Jane Does?"

"No," Robin hesitated and then sheepishly said,

"I forgot to ask. Maybe because subconsciously, I didn't want to go there."

"What do you mean Jane Does?" Marie poked her head into the kitchen.

"When you call emergency rooms on the chance that a person could be unconscious or unable to give their name, an unidentifiable man is called a John Doe, and an unidentifiable woman will be labeled a Jane Doe," Sandy explained.

This was news to Marie, but since Robin was in the medical field, she already knew this.

Marie went into the living room and sat down as people began to file inside.

"I just asked for Bella by name." Robin clenched her jaw, knowing that as a nurse, this was something she should have considered. Robin's face grew pale and taut. The truth was, asking for unidentified women meant that they were also looking for an unconscious or dead woman, and she hadn't allowed her thoughts to go there. "Do you have any recent close-up photos of Bella?" "Yeah, I'll go get them," Robin said.

Rather than waiting in the kitchen, Sandy followed Robin down the hallway until they were out of earshot of her friends.

Drawing close to Robin, Sandy lowered her voice and asked one final question. "Forgive me for being so personal, but do you two share a sexual relationship, and if so, are there any problems with the sex?"

Robin pulled back a little, smiled stiffly, and then answered. "Yes, we share a sexual relationship, and no, there haven't been any problems. Our sex life has always been good. She didn't run off with someone else if that's what you're thinking."

"Sorry, but I had to ask. I try not to leave any

stones unturned. I hope you understand that."

Robin hesitated, relaxed a little, and then answered, "Yes, I do…and thanks for being here."

Sandy then strode back to the cramped living room to address the group. "Okay, I have two leads that I'm going to check out myself," she said. "First, I'm going to check for unidentified women that might've come into the emergency room. Then I'm going to check out Starbucks where Bella likes to hang out. For the rest of you, this is what I suggest: Bella is missing along with her car. It's often easier to find a car than to find a person. Fortunately, Bella's car is a bit easier to spot than most because it's red, and it has a rainbow decal on the back window. It's a Toyota Corolla. The license plate number is ABL-6719. I would like two people to volunteer to check the closest park. I would like you to walk all over every square inch of it, but please, only do this in pairs and only during daylight hours. For safety, it's important for you to stay together. If you find anything at all, do not touch it or even walk around it. Just back off and call me right away. Do not disturb anything. Do you understand?"

The women and gay men present understood well that Sandy was suggesting that they could disturb a crime scene where a rape or murder may have taken place. In response, volunteers looked down or swallowed hard. There was a low murmur of assent. Yes, they understood.

"Okay," Sandy said while pointing at two women. "Will you two go check out the closest park? I would also like two people to check dead-end streets around here and behind businesses, especially parking lots and around that big industrial park. Okay, you and you!"

Marie looked at the familiar face of her cousin.

"Marie and Squeaky, I want you two to go over to the parking lot where Bella works, look for her car, and even if it isn't there, walk every square inch of the lot and see if you can find anything suspicious. Now I would like four of you to carry pictures of Bella around to the people at local businesses and to talk with people you meet that are running around outside in this area. Tell them she has disappeared and ask if anyone remembers seeing her."

As luck would have it, Sandy hit paydirt on the first place she checked. Bella's Toyota sat undisturbed in the side parking lot at Starbucks. She called Robin at once.

"Robin? This is Detective LePersiller, er, Sandy," she said. "We didn't find Bella," she began cautiously, "but we did find her car."

"What? Where?"

"It's in the Starbucks parking lot. It's locked up tight. I don't see any obvious signs of foul play," she said.

"I'm coming," Robin said.

"Okay, if you like, but do me a favor and bring a key to her car if you have an extra."

Robin hung up and called Marie. Having failed to find Bella's car in the employee lot of Jolly Rancher, her two friends had left there and were in the process of searching surrounding areas. The instant they heard that Bella's car had been found, Marie flipped a U-turn, and they headed straight for Robin and Bella's house.

"Robin, hold tight," Marie calmly ordered over the phone. "Squeaky and I will pick you up and drive you to Starbucks."

Robin then called Bella's sister, who was in the process of printing more fliers and getting a babysitter lined up for her children so she could come stay. "Bonita, they found Bella's car."

By the time Squeaky, Marie, and Robin arrived at Starbucks, it was still too early to file an official police report. Sandy had not called in a police locksmith but instead waited for Robin to show up with the key.

Strangely, the minute she took hold of the key, Sandy didn't unlock the door. Instead, she walked over and spoke quietly to Squeaky and Marie. Like most long-term couples whose movements often were in unison, shoulder-to-shoulder Squeaky and Marie walked straight to Robin and explained that they needed to clear the area.

As Robin dutifully followed her friends, the horrible truth didn't sink in right away. At first, she assumed that Sandy just wanted them to stay out of the crime scene. But when Sandy headed to the back of the car, it suddenly occurred to Robin that the reason her friends led her away was that no one wanted her to be there when the trunk was opened. With fear gripping the pit of her stomach, Robin realized that this seasoned detective knew there was a chance that Bella's body could be in the trunk of her own car.

Robin, whose actions were stoic up to that point, collapsed against Marie. "Oh, my God. don't let it be," she pleaded. "Please don't let her be dead!"

"I don't think she's dead," Squeaky said with a clear and calm voice.

"What?"

"She's not in that trunk, and she's not dead," Squeaky announced with a tone of authority.

Marie and Robin turned to face Squeaky together.

Squeaky's blue eyes were as clear as ever, and her face was almost serene. She looked at the pair and waved her arms in a dismissive manner. They both knew that at times, Squeaky's psychic abilities were eerily right.

"Well, hell, if you know that," Robin snapped at her, "then ask the spirits where Bella is at!"

"I'm sorry. I don't know that. I wish I did. The only thing that has come to me is the certainty that she's not dead."

Marie protectively pulled Squeaky to her side, looked at Robin, and said, "Yeah, well, at least that's something positive."

Chapter Twelve: Detective P Opens the Trunk

Saturday, October 9

Detective P did not like opening trunks. She knew officers who felt it a routine procedure, but for her, opening a trunk was a horror that often replayed itself in recurrent nightmares. Her traumatic incident happened when she was a young and inexperienced detective. Tagging along with a seasoned veteran of the police force, the two of them came to a stop at the back of a suspect's car. She noticed her male cohort's face had gone grim, but she didn't know why, and she didn't sniff the air for odor as he had. She fully expected the trunk they were about to open would be cluttered with junk or filled with stolen goods. She was even a little excited about clues the car might hold, but she tempered that thought with the realization that this could be another dead end. That was all she expected.

Sandy still had clear images of the grim-faced veteran officer as he turned the key and, using a handkerchief to keep his fingerprints from contaminating the scene, carefully lifted the navy-blue trunk lid on its far-left edge. Then the two officers' actions differed; as the experienced officer was quietly moving backward, Sandy eagerly stepped forward. In her mind, their search for clues was something like a scavenger hunt with this vehicle providing them with more information. The grisly gray and white-faced body of the young woman that greeted them was the last thing she had expected. The ghastly thing in the trunk before them was a person, Sandy knew it was a person, yet it was not. Because no human being was all gray and white like that and so unnaturally folded up. It was in that flash of surprise that she involuntarily drew in a deep breath of air, the same foul air suddenly released from a confined space and filled with the putrid stench of death. The rotted odor was so horrible that she had stumbled backward, then gagged repeatedly, with vomit threatening but not coming up.

Later, the seasoned detective apologized to her. He thought he smelled the faintest scent of death, which was why he had been cautious, but he didn't really expect to find a body. He was a decent man, fatherly to her in a tough guy kind of way, and he wanted her to know that he wouldn't have thrown that in her face had he known what was in store for them.

That experience, as with other grisly ordeals that police officers and detectives had to face, robbed Detective Sandy LePersiller of innocence and replaced it with a certain degree of caution and cynicism. As a detective, she accepted this change because it came with the job.

Now with a missing person in the lesbian community and another unopened trunk looming before her, Sandy cautiously sniffed the air as she bent over the closed trunk while pretending to inspect the license plate. There was no odor.

As she slipped the key into the lock, her palms sweat, and her heart pounded in her throat, and she felt terribly alone. One of the problems with being a detective was that sometimes she was forced to be a tough guy even when she didn't feel like a tough guy. "It sure would be nice," she mumbled quietly, "if one of my buddies was here with me now." Sandy took one last look around to make certain that neither Robin nor her friends were within viewing sight, then slowly lifted the dreaded trunk lid and found, to her great relief, that it was empty.

Chapter Thirteen: Crime Recorded on Videotape?

Early Saturday afternoon, October 9

Detective Persevere became excited when she learned that Starbucks had a security system that included video monitoring of their parking lot. Unfortunately, her excitement took a nosedive when the manager discovered that the camera was defective. Sandy often had to face the sad fact that not all security systems were well kept. It was human nature to forget about automatic cameras until needed, and then, it was too late.

Gradual Freedom

Late Saturday morning, October 9

"Salvia, I have to pee!" Bella said.

Obviously expecting such a request, Sal brought over Bella's clothing, untied the leather straps from the padded restraints attached to her ankles, and then put on Bella's jeans she had previously removed. All the while, Bella's hands remained firmly secured. Sal then attached a short piece of chain between the two ankle restraints and locked this in place with a small padlock. Next, she untied the straps holding Bella's hands, then stepped back and handed over her blouse and bra.

Sal smiled briefly. "Now stand up and hold out your hands."

Bella scooted off the bed and stood, facing Sal. As

she stood, Bella noted that Sal was about four inches taller than her. With Sal watching her every move, Bella considered turning around as she put her bra on. Since there was nothing that Sal had not already seen, she decided against it. Bella quietly threaded the straps of her wrist restraints through her bra and then through both of her sleeves.

"Hold out your hands," Salvia repeated quietly.

Bella did as she was told and watched as Sal attached the leather straps from her wrist restraints to the foot chain. She would now be able to use her hands, which she would need when going to the bathroom, but the way Salvia had tied her prevented her from being able to bring her hands above the level of her waist unless both knees were slightly bent. She recognized this as a clever plan because it enabled Bella to move around freely, but it restricted her ability to fight or run.

"You probably roped calves in the rodeo," Bella said dryly.

Sal grinned. "Not unless you're calling yourself a little heifer." She then pointed and said,

"There's a chemical flush toilet over there in the corner."

Afterward, Salvia tossed Bella a wet washcloth to wash her hands and cooked their lunch.

The two of them ate in near silence.

"My partner, Robin, probably called the cops by now," Bella finally said.

"Yeah, I figured that," Salvia said with a dismissive gesture, "but they'll never find us."

Bella leaned forward. "Salvia, I know this is what you think you want, but this will never work."

"Why not?"

"Because you aren't considering my feelings, that's why. I don't want to be here."

Salvia softened her voice. "Things will get better, I promise. You'll change your mind."

"No, I won't. I won't ever change my mind. Please, don't do this. Just let me go,

Salvia…please."

"Look, I'm going to treat you well, but you need to learn what subjects to avoid. This is one of them. Talk like that again, and I'll give you plenty of time to reconsider."

But Bella didn't quiet down; instead, she raised her voice and continued the argument.

Suddenly, Salvia slammed her fist so hard on the table that the dishes and silverware rattled. Bella winced.

"Okay, that's it!" Salvia shot back. "I warned you! Now get over here!"

But Bella didn't move. Wordlessly, Salvia strode over, grabbed her by one arm, and easily dragged her to a metal loop welded to the wall near the toilet. She then snapped a handcuff over Bella's left wrist and attached the other end to the metal loop. Once Bella was securely fastened to the wall, Sal snatched her coat off a rack and stormed out the door. She didn't come back for eight long hours.

Chapter Fourteen: Robin's Thoughts

Saturday afternoon, October 9

Robin felt that finding Bella's car was a mixed blessing. Optimistically, she thought the discovery would cause the police to realize someone had taken Bella. Although Bella's car was of interest to Sandy, she pointed out that Bella could have willingly gone off with another person.

It was a pity that Sandy didn't know Bella better. Bella was a communicative person who, even when angry, could never keep away from Robin for long. She was dependable. She texted or called home often. Fifteen hours passing without Robin hearing a single word from Bella meant that something was terribly wrong.

The car was also a disturbing find because it shot to hell the story Robin had fabricated in her mind. No longer could she believe that Bella somehow suffered a head injury, developed amnesia, and accidentally drove off to another state. Nor was Bella involved in an accident. Discovery of the vehicle meant that Bella was out there somewhere without her car. Even if she had wandered off on her own, they now knew she was not in her Toyota and could be on foot. To Robin, the idea of Bella walking around alone and confused, day and night, was unsettling. At five feet one inch tall and one hundred eighteen pounds, she would be easy to overpower.

❧❧❧❧

While Robin's thoughts on finding Bella faltered, Marie's plans gained momentum. Marie decided to organize women with dog teams, and she encouraged the women to check out vacant and neglected properties, sheds, ditches, weed patches, and areas along rivers and streams within a five-mile radius of Starbucks.

She didn't wish to criticize their efforts, but Robin didn't believe the places her friends were checking were at all promising. To her, the idea of using untrained dogs and searching vacant property suggested they were looking for a dead body instead of a live person. When she voiced this fear, her friends cited examples of kidnapped people who were found alive in sheds and vacant buildings. They also told Robin that there was always a chance that the police might catch whoever was responsible, if only through a routine traffic stop. Miracles did happen, and a miracle was what they were praying for.

❧❧❧❧

Late that night, Bella's car was hauled off to a crime lab. Detective LePersiller said one of the first things the lab did was to dust the car for fingerprints. She was told that so far, the only identifiable prints belonged to Robin and Bella. Then, it was discovered that the coil pack on the engine was loose. The police said it appeared as if it had been tampered with. That didn't make sense to Robin because the car was locked. When Bella's car was locked, no one could get under the hood. Robin thought it more likely that the coil pack had jiggled loose. Regardless of the reason her car wouldn't start, the fact that it did falter could have put Bella in touch with someone offering to help. Robin sensed that the police believed this meant that Bella was taken by someone who knew her.

Chapter Fifteen: Shackled and Alone

Saturday afternoon, October 9

Since Bella had made Salvia angry enough to leave her alone, Bella tried to use the first few hours of her solitude productively. She pulled and twisted at the handcuffs, and she tugged and kicked at the metal ring that held her firmly to the wall. She looked around for a bobby pin or tiny object that she might use to pick the lock on the handcuffs. But nothing useful was within her limited reach. The cold handcuffs and metal loop were solid, and they held firm.

She studied every feature inside the Quonset hut confining her. And just in case such knowledge might prove useful, she committed to memory every detail within her view. After that, she tried to find a weakness in the structure. Unfortunately, she didn't find herself in a promising situation. This industrial-type building was solidly built, and judging from the total lack of vehicle and human noise in the area, it was also extremely isolated.

Bella searched her mind for every useful bit of knowledge she might have accidentally learned about hostage situations. Too bad she had never received any formal training on the subject. She had gathered a good deal of her education about crime from television shows and movies she had seen. If she remembered correctly, a hostage was supposed to remain agreeable and talk to their captor. Becoming better acquainted was supposed to increase one's chance of survival. It only made sense that earning Salvia's trust would increase her chance of escape.

Hours crept by, and Bella ran out of productive ideas. No longer was she able to remain in a logical or practical frame of mind. Although only one of her limbs was fastened to the wall, in some ways, it had been more comfortable to be tied to the bed. Now the portable toilet was her only seat.

When the last rays of sunlight disappeared, so did Bella's firm resolve. Only when her optimism failed her did she finally allow the raw edge of emotion to overwhelm her senses.

In the quiet solitude, Bella allowed herself to mull over the darkest thoughts possible. Salvia was so crazy she might just leave her here to die, or she might come back, strip off her clothes, and tie her across the bed in four-point restraints again. Salvia had such an unstable temper that she might hold a pillow over Bella's face again, only the next time, she might hold it down for so long that Bella might never breathe again.

Bella imagined her lifeless body, found naked and spread-eagle for all the male cops to witness and to joke about, a horrible scene destined to be photographed from every angle. Not a quiet death with dignity, but a senseless cruelty preserved forever in ghastly photos that might someday be used in a public trial. Shocking photos of her naked body to be passed around by well-dressed and respectable people serving as jurors, shamed, even after death. Thanks to technology, cruelty would be brought home in the stark detail of black and white, or in bloody color, so visceral that her family and friends might never be able to erase such a picture from their minds.

In such a situation, it was possible that in the end, Bella might not be remembered for her laughter or the acts of kindness that she had spent a lifetime performing, but instead, memories of her might consist of nothing but the fact that her life was senselessly taken and that the last moments she experienced were those of torturous abandonment.

Unleashing her tears, Bella placed her face on her knees and sobbed uncontrollably. She cried, first for herself, then for everyone else: Robin, Rusty, and her family, all of whom she might never see again. When she didn't think there was anything left to cry about, Bella cried because she did not get an opportunity to say goodbye to Robin. She had barely finished crying when she heard Sal's truck and then the lock clattering against the metal door. Finally, Salvia reappeared, and with her came hope.

Chapter Sixteen: In Too Deep

Late Saturday evening, October 9

Salvia hadn't given it a great deal of thought, but the view that greeted her when she stepped in the door was heart-wrenching. Bella was sitting on the floor, still firmly handcuffed to the wall. Her beautiful hair was disheveled, her eyes reddened, and her cheeks wet with tears. She did notice a glimmer of recognition, and even a hint that Bella was glad to see her, but this, she knew, was born of loneliness and desperation. It was not the sincere welcome she hoped would someday greet her.

Not only had she made this beautiful woman terribly unhappy for the moment, but it caused Salvia to wonder just what would happen if Bella was right. What if Bella never grew to care for her? The truth was, if she could not win this woman's affection, then her actions of the past twenty-four hours were nothing but a series of mistakes and surely the worst kind of mistakes, too, because they were not the kind of thing she could take back.

I can't just go and return a kidnapped person. But then again, that was not technically correct. Such things had been done before. She once saw a true-life TV program about the men who kidnapped Frank Sinatra's son. They intended to kill him, but one of his kidnappers took pity and returned the boy close to his home.

Salvia knew that returning a kidnapped person would practically guarantee exposure and shame, which was likely to be closely followed by an escort straight to prison. If she remembered the story correctly, that was what had happened to the man who was kindest to Sinatra's son. His sentence was lighter than his cohorts, but lighter or not, a prison sentence was still a prison sentence!

Thoughts about her father popped into Salvia's head. She remembered him admitting there were times in his life when he had gotten himself in too deep. When this happened, he claimed he just shrugged and said, "Oh, well, in for a penny, in for a pound." Her father's advice to her was that when there was no ability to back out of a situation, the best course of action was to make the most of it. Salvia knew that she had placed herself in just such a situation.

She removed the handcuffs and asked Bella to sit at the table. Bella sat quietly at the table while Salvia turned on the radio and made dinner. When she sat down, to her relief, Bella became talkative and pleasant.

Just before midnight, the police officially opened the missing persons case on Isabella Sanchez, and Detective P was assigned as the lead detective.

Marie and Squeaky

Sunday, October 10

Marie and Squeaky got Rusty under the pretense of taking the dog for a walk. Their real purpose in borrowing the dog was because Marie believed a woman's own dog was far more likely to find her mistress than any of her human friends. Compared to a human's, a dog's sense of smell was between ten thousand and one hundred thousand times better. Bella's dog sniffed the coffeehouse's side door with interest, sniffed the sidewalk, walked a short distance from the door to a spot in the Starbucks parking lot, and then stopped cold, as if her mistress's scent had vanished.

Marie and Squeaky stood quietly and looked at each other. An untrained dog was not much to go on, but Sandy could be right. Because if Bella had gone off with someone else, the trail would indeed have been a short one.

After searching around the grounds of the coffeehouse, Robin's friends decided to try another area. They left Starbucks and headed for a local greenbelt, which was public land along Clear Creek River. If they found nothing, which was what Squeaky predicted, at least they had done something other than worrying uselessly.

Marie looked at Squeaky. "Now that Sandy got herself assigned to Bella's case, I have a good feeling."

"Yeah?" Squeaky said. "I hope you're right. What do you think makes Sandy such a

resolute detective?"

"I don't know, maybe it comes from the weird relationship she has with Birdie."

"What's so weird about it?"

"Haven't I told you?"

"No, you haven't. What?"

"They never have sex," Marie explained.

"What? You've got to be kidding. Never?"

"Nope. Never. It's an asexual relationship."

"Then why did Sandy get together with Birdie in the first place?" Squeaky asked. "Have they tried counseling?"

"No, Sandy says that Birdie just doesn't want to have sex, period."

"Ah, gee, then I just wouldn't want to stay with her, period."

"Yeah, well, neither would I," Marie said, "but Sandy says they worked it out."

"How?" Squeaky demanded. "How the hell do you work out something like that?"

"Um, well, I don't think Sandy wants this advertised, but they have an open relationship."
"Really?"

"Yeah, but that hasn't worked out too well for Sandy. None of the women she finds on the side ever seem to last long," Marie said.

"I can just imagine."

"The problem is that every time it seems like she's found someone who claims to understand that Sandy loves Birdie and intends to stay with her, the new woman goes and falls in love with Sandy anyway. Sandy's women either leave in disappointment or they try to sabotage

Sandy's relationship with Birdie so that Sandy will move in with them."

"Women are like that," Squeaky said. "They don't usually make good fuck buddies."

Marie nodded in agreement. "Also, the whole time that Sandy is getting a little on the side—whenever she's that lucky—Birdie tells her that her 'whoring friends' can't call their house. She gives her one day a week, and that's it. Plus, she tries to make Sandy feel guilty for what Birdie pushed her into doing in the first place."

"Shit, that woman has got some kind of hang-up!"

"Yeah," Marie agreed, "but, according to Sandy, she treats her well in every other aspect.

Intimacy and sex are just things she won't do."

"Well, what the hell else is there?" Squeaky said.

"Oh, don't be silly. You know...being there for you when you're sick, helping around the house, buying you things, backing you up, and all that kind of stuff."

"I suppose."

"Sandy hardly ever has anyone to be intimate with, so she tries to choke back her sex drive. She mostly lives a lie by trying to pretend that her need for sex doesn't exist. All the while, she has this misplaced loyalty thing for Birdie. But even with all that, I don't think Sandy will ever leave Birdie, no matter how hard it is for her to survive like that. She'll just work a lot."

"Yeah, it looks to me like she pours her heart and soul into her work." Squeaky nodded in agreement.

"Yep. Those guys that first called her Lady Persevere didn't know how right they were." "Or maybe," Squeaky said, "they do know."

Chapter Seventeen: Detective P Gets Sidetracked

Sunday, October 10

Late Sunday, Sandy finished the paperwork, drove home, and quietly entered her house, so as not to awaken Birdie. She then carefully considered her investigative abilities. She knew one reason for her success was due to unconventional actions. For example, she sometimes asked family and relatives for limited help. Requesting help outside of the police department was not standard procedure and for good reason; some people had a way of interfering with an investigation more than they contributed. In addition, whenever lay people were involved, it invariably meant she would have to run down useless leads and receive annoying telephone calls at odd hours.

Her gambling that she would receive help by select people often paid off. Why shouldn't involving loved ones be useful? Who else cares more than family and friends? Why should I settle for one pair of eyes during one part of the day when it is possible to have multiple pairs of eyes around the clock?

Sandy was proud of her cousin Marie and intrigued by Squeaky's intuitive prediction.

Whether it made sense or not, Squeaky's psychic claim that Bella was still alive was reassuring.

Since Sandy and her partner, Bernadette, had

separate bedrooms, Sandy was lying in her lonesome bed, staring at the ceiling when she concluded that someone had lured Isabella Sanchez into their own car—of that much she was certain. But how was she going to find out what this unknown person looked like, and how would she learn about the type and color of their vehicle?

≈≈≈

Early Monday, October 11

When the phone rang in the middle of the night, Sandy instinctively reached for it, assuming it had something to do with work. The caller asked for Birdie. She set the receiver on her bedside table and headed upstairs to Birdie's room. The two women soon learned that Birdie's mother had passed away, and this, Sandy quickly realized, put her in an awkward position. She didn't want her boss to take her off this missing person case, but she felt obligated to go with Birdie to her mother's funeral in Georgia. She knew that if she were straight, she could be honest with her employers, and such truth would be met with sympathy and understanding. But her circumstances were different. She was not "out" at work, and she didn't wish for this bump in the road to force an official outing.

Besides, even if she did out herself, there still was no guarantee they would excuse her to attend a funeral for her roommate's mother. So, the official reason she devised was that Birdie's mother was her own Aunt Carol, who had been like a grandmother to her. This, of course, was a gamble because aunts didn't qualify for bereavement leave. The department reluctantly allowed her to take the time off.

Though her supervisor excused her, it was clear he disapproved of her leave. The minute she was gone, he appointed Detective Raymond Spears to her missing person case as the lead detective.

⊱⊰⊱⊰

Monday night, October 11

Every night Bella spent in captivity was a long one. So, to prevent depression and boredom, she allowed her mind to take her back to previous life experiences. In this case, she thought about mental disorders. Robin once told her about a conversation that occurred between two patients in the psych ward who were not aware that Robin could hear them.

1st: "Keep clear of that new patient over there, she's crazy as a bedbug."

2nd: "I doubt if a bedbug is crazy. Bedbugs know exactly what they want and usually how to get there, too!"

1st: "Yep. Most of us with mental problems know exactly what we want, too. Only trouble is, we can't figure out how to get there!"

2nd: "So I guess that makes those bugs a damn sight smarter than us!" Then the women laughed at themselves and their situation.

Robin said the psych ward was not ideal for her as a nurse because she lacked the necessary patience it required. She claimed it took too long for people with mental problems to get well. Robin described her favorite patient as a man who comes in, has surgery, gets well fast, and goes home.

But Bella was unlike Robin in this respect. She knew she was a far more patient person. Bella thought of the mind as a labyrinth that could become twisted, but unless it was permanently damaged or diseased, she believed problems of the mind were temporary states of existence, conditions that therapy and medications could eventually restore.

In Bella's present situation, she had no way of knowing if anyone would ever find her. She also didn't know if she and Salvia would both survive, but she did know that if by miracle or good fortune they did make it, she would like to see Salvia get the help she needed and make the journey toward wellness.

Chapter Eighteen : Three Women Reacting Differently

Tuesday, October 12

On Tuesday and Wednesday, Bella began working harder to make Salvia and her shared time together more pleasant. To pass the time, they played games and read books. But there were a couple of subjects Bella carefully avoided to prevent any future outbursts, including their relationship, or lack thereof.

Wednesday, October 13

Robin was not doing well. So far, she had accidentally set the smoke alarm off twice and, had it not been for her guests, she would have flooded the bathroom by overfilling the tub. She was calling in sick one day at a time when a fellow nurse called and advised her to take a leave of absence because she had overheard the administration saying they might have to fire her. That was all it took to set Robin into a full-blown fury. Her home health company had been kind and understanding, but the hospital had foolishly decided to push on a person who was already balancing on a ledge. Robin intended to grab her wallet and keys and march into her hospital and give them a piece of her mind, but she couldn't find her wallet or her keys.

Bella's sister Bonita took charge. She possessed the same calming influence on Robin as Bella. When Bonita found the keys, Robin made no attempt to take them away "This is no time for you to be driving, my love," said Bonita as she looked her in the eyes. "And I think you should let me do all the talking at your hospital too." Robin mutely nodded.

A Detective at Work
Thursday, October 14

When the funeral for Birdie's mother was over, Sandy returned to duty. But when she learned her lead position was given away, she was angry. Her supervisor allowed her to remain on the case, but there was no way in hell she should have lost the primary position, especially not to someone like Randy Spears, who didn't work well with others. The entire fiasco incensed Robin and her friends. Unfortunately, there was nothing that she—their favorite detective—could do about it.

Spears informed Detective P that the lab had lifted a print from Bella's Toyota that didn't belong to Robin or Bella. But so far, the crime lab had not matched it to any on file. They both knew it was possible for fingerprints on the outside of a car to belong to anyone who happened to be passing through a parking lot, and they might not mean a thing. More importantly, Spears noted there was recent activity on the missing woman's credit card, and they had obtained a poor-quality video of what Spears described as "the stupid bastard that used the card."

Sandy studied the convenience store video but said little. Overall, it was disappointing to her because she had hoped for signs of Bella and saw none and because the person using the credit card was so nondescript that it wasn't helpful. However, one difference between the thinking of Detective Spears and Detective P was that Spears assumed the credit card user in the video was a man, while Sandy left the possibility open that the person could be a butch woman, particularly because this person was not very tall.

❧ ❧ ❧ ❧

Sandy questioned the employees at Starbucks, but no one remembered seeing Bella. Although her investigation had stalled, this did not deter Lady Persevere. She questioned other people in the area, and at the risk of appearing to be the stereotypical coffee-drinking, doughnut-eating cop with nothing better to do, she hung around Starbucks for hours on end, eager to talk to every customer who walked in the door. I am not giving up because eventually, someone will remember Bella.

A case like this could be very frustrating. Bella's partner, family, and friends wanted answers, and they wanted them now. At this very moment, Bella could be God only knew where lying injured or hanging on to life by a thread. They had lost precious time, and the pressure was mounting for her to produce answers. At this very moment, the good detective had next to nothing.

Sandy doggedly continued questioning customers at Starbucks until she finally happened upon an older woman who distinctly remembered seeing Bella leave the store with a young man with a limp. The older woman said the two of them appeared comfortable with each other and that the man tried to help her fix her car. She described the man as a short, stocky Caucasian with medium-length brown hair. This sounded like the man on their credit card video. This sole eyewitness could recall that and nothing more. Detective P thanked the woman, pressed one of her cards into her hand, and asked her to call if she remembered anything else.

That evening, her witness called to say, "I didn't see the man get in or out of it, but I just remembered that a blue Jeep parked in the lot when I came in, and it was gone when I went out. There were so few customers in the shop at the time that I think it's likely that the Jeep belonged to him."

It was not the strongest of leads, but in Sandy's mind, it was a lead worthy of investigation.

When Sandy told Spears about the Jeep, he said, "If you want to waste your time on a wild goose chase, don't let me stand in your way. Knock yourself out, Detective!"

Sandy had walked part way down the hall when she overheard Spears's lowered voice as he spoke to one of his few friends in the department. "That ought to keep her out of my hair for a while."

"You horse's ass," Sandy muttered to herself as she struck the door. "You stay out of my hair, and I'll gladly stay out of yours!"

She decided to sort through Jeeps owned by people who lived within a five-mile radius of Starbucks but soon realized this was a time-consuming task.

Chapter Nineteen : Long Captivity

Thursday, October 14

Although she was not particularly a fan of television, Bella found herself wishing for a TV program or for any diversion whenever their conversations ran dry. Fortunately, Salvia stepped up to the plate by handing Bella an old magazine that she asked her to read aloud. Bella gladly read to Sal. Not only did she want to combat her own boredom, but she considered it crucial to keep Salvia as happy and stable as possible. She tried to buy enough time for the authorities to track her down.

Bella read for a long time, then set the magazine down, looked at Salvia, and casually said, "Tell me about your family. What was your father like?"

Salvia smiled. "You first," she said. "I'll bet you had a nice father. You have good memories to share, don't you?"

Now it was Bella's turn to smile. She certainly did!

"Well," she began slowly, "when we were little, my dad used to bounce us on his knee. Sometimes, we played airplane, and he swung us around in circles. My dad was a big guy, so when he took us for piggyback rides, it was great fun because we were so high up that we could touch the ceiling. Back then, he seemed like a giant to me. When we got a little bigger, he held our feet up in the air while we walked around with our hands. We called it playing wheelbarrow. Whenever we were around traffic, he held our hands and watched us real close, and he took us on lots of vacations."

"What kind of places did you go to?" Salvia asked.

"Wow, we went to a whole bunch of places! We went to Disneyland and Yellowstone and to the ocean off California."

"What kinds of things did he say to you?" Salvia asked.

"Well, sometimes he said things that did not make sense to me when I was little. But I knew even then that something was wrong—wrong enough for me to remember it—and when I got older, I was able to put it all together."

"Like what?"

"One day, he came home and started ranting and raving about parked cars. He said everyone should have a driveway, and no one should be allowed to park on the street. To us, all his talk about driveways and parked cars just came out of the blue, yet he was very passionate about it. That's why I remembered it. It wasn't until years later that I found out that one evening when he was a volunteer police officer, he attended the scene of an accident where a child was run over by a car and killed. A girl ran out from between two parked cars, and the driver hadn't seen her in time and couldn't help what happened. It wasn't his fault that the child died, but he was devastated."

"Oh, that must've been hard for your dad, too."
"Yeah, I think it was," Bella agreed.

"What else did he say when you were little?"

"When we were kids, we always yelled, 'Daddy's home!' then all three of us would race to his car door. We ran so fast that we were already there before he could get his door open. But when we got a little older, he came home one day while we were playing outside, and we all looked up but none of us raced to see him anymore. Dad got out of his car and lowered his voice and said, 'I can remember when you kids were glad to see me.' We knew he was disappointed, and we felt bad because we didn't mean to hurt his feelings."

Salvia was listening carefully, so Bella continued. "When I got older, I realized that not all fathers were as interested in their children as my dad was. He told me a father's love is the most perfect love in the world because mothers tend to get jealous. Most people would say mothers are more important, but my dad said all a father wants is for his children to be happy. I've often thought about his words. That was when I realized how much he loved me. My dad was an extremely cautious man, and he was always careful not to get himself hurt, but I believe with all my heart that he would have given his right arm to protect us."

The two women sat in comfortable silence. Bella sighed and finally said, "Okay, your turn."

"Uh, not much to say, really," Salvia said. "My dad wanted me to be his little boy. We fixed cars when I was little, but when I hit puberty, he got distant..." Salvia trailed off.

Bella studied Salvia's face.

"I don't know why he did the things he did," Salvia said. "He should have stood up to my mother, but he wanted peace so bad that he let my mom push him around. When I reached my rebellious years, I started to fight with my mother. I always thought he should have, too. I wanted him to stand up for himself, but he didn't. He was a wimp. He thought he was doing the right thing, but neither one of us—my mom or I—respected him for it." "I'm sorry," Bella said. "I wish you could've had a dad like mine." "Me too," Salvia said.

Bella chastised herself for talking so much about her dad. Perhaps if she'd known what Salvia's father was like, she may have toned down her enthusiasm a little. Now she felt guilty. But on the other hand, everything she said was the truth, and the truth was never wrong. Her dad had been a good father, and considering her present situation, Bella thought that she might be joining her dad in the afterlife sooner than expected.

❧❧❧❧

That night, Bella lay quietly in the darkness, her mind roving freely.

Her thoughts revolved around Robin. How cruel it was to keep her in the dark! Robin would have no idea what happened to her; she wouldn't know exactly when Bella disappeared, where she was, or even that she was still alive and very much in love with her.

Oh, honey, how I wish I could slip away and talk to you, if only for a moment. Bella wondered about ongoing efforts to find her. Has Robin been lucky enough to collaborate with people who listened to her? Did they find my car? Did they discover the purchase Salvia made on my credit card? I wonder if I can get Salvia to make a second purchase. If she does, I hope to God the police notice it, and I hope it'll lead them to this place…wherever the hell I am!

Chapter Twenty: Robin's Frustration

Thursday morning, October 14

Robin felt like an empty shell. She walked around in a daze with a mind full of unanswered questions. Why did Bella disappear? What happened to her? Where is she? And why can't they find her? Robin wondered if there was anything she could be doing that she wasn't already doing, and she thought about the most dreaded possibility of all. What am I going to do if they never find her?

Unfortunately, there were no answers. There was no such thing as an omnipotent detective or a magic wizard. Not even all the high-tech gadgets of the day were helping them out. Here Robin was, feeling like her world had been knocked off its foundation, yet she sensed this new detective named Randy Spears viewed her case as just another missing woman, just one more file to clutter up his desk. She'd often heard that a person's every step was being videotaped or watched, but now that she found herself in the position of hoping she could receive help from all these prying electronic eyes, there didn't seem to be a single one that was helping them learn what happened to Bella.

Robin developed new sympathy for patients' families, those stunned by recent turns of events and frustrated by professionals who had no answers. She sympathized with the haunted look of those on television who begged for information as to the location of lost loved ones. She now recognized their situation for what it truly was: a haunting and painfully slow form of torture.

Robin fought hard to hold on to certain beliefs yet vacillated in the effort. She overheard the statement that no one really knows what goes on in the heart of another. She also heard it implied that an affair was in the making. For the briefest of moments, those opinions caused doubt to rear its ugly head. But then Robin resolved that her relationship with Bella was an exception because they knew each other so well. Although she felt certain that Bella would never willingly hop into a stranger or a semi-stranger's car, it looked like that was exactly what Bella had done. How could she blame her? One of the things she loved best about Bella was her friendly and trusting manner. When she thought back, Bella had taken in hitchhikers in the past. Robin also found it troubling that Bella had never mentioned any men in her life, but Sandy now had an eyewitness who claimed that Bella appeared "very comfortable" in the company of a man at Starbucks.

Could Bella be a closet bisexual? If she was, Robin wished Bella had told her. Now if the authorities wound up finding Bella snuggled happily in the arms of a man, Robin would feel humiliated and deceived. Her heart would surely break!

She didn't know, damn it! Nor could she figure it out. That was what the police were for, she told herself. The cops were working on it. Unfortunately, they had few clues to go on, and now Robin didn't even know what to make of the detectives! After Robin had bestowed complete faith in Detective Sandy LePersiller, for reasons she would never know, Sandy's superior chose to demote her from the lead position. Still, Robin knew that cops could be incredibly sexist and even stupid at times. Certainly, her first impression of Detective Spears was proof of that.

Follow-up Work
Thursday afternoon, October 14

With little to go on, Sandy decided to return to Bella and Robin's home for a more informal visit. Over the years, she had discovered that more casual and less stressful visits tended to expose minute details which, on occasion, had proved extremely valuable to a case. Sandy approached Robin, hoping for useful information. She was not expecting to meet anyone who would inexplicably draw her attention, such as Robin's friend Avery.

In her quest for more information, the persistent detective carefully questioned Robin about Bella's disappearance once more. She wasn't really getting anything new or useful, but Sandy accepted that was sometimes how things went. Her mind was on the details of her work when she suddenly sensed that someone was behind her. Instinctively, she swung around and visibly jumped up in her chair only to discover that this perceived threat turned out to be one of Robin's houseguests. The embarrassment of jumping to conclusions caused her to feel a warm flush climbing up her face.

"Whoa, Detective, are you always this tense?" the woman asked.

"Only when folks sneak up on me," Sandy replied.

Glancing from one woman to the other, Robin introduced them. Both women noticed that Robin informally introduced the detective by referring to her as Sandy. Avery straightened her sleek body, which she had draped against a corner. Her careful grin and flirtatious green eyes openly roved Sandy's body. The two women shook each other's hands, which was something Sandy performed often and automatically in her work. In this instance, she felt vaguely uncomfortable. The soft flesh of Avery's hand was at odds with her inappropriately strong grip, and while the pumping action of their handshake soon ended, their strong grasp lingered.

Although Robin appeared oblivious to their continued hold, Sandy believed that Avery's actions suggested something beyond a formal introduction. She recognized a challenge of sorts—a display of strength to exert supremacy. Sandy couldn't suppress a wry grin, for Avery was obviously challenging the wrong woman. Sandy knew this was something Avery might not have attempted if she'd known about Sandy's weight training. Smiling cautiously, Sandy eyed the slender and graceful woman before her. Avery was not a small woman, yet she was dwarfed by Sandy, who had the advantage of greater height and muscle mass.

The truth was that Sandy was modestly proud of her own physique, even though the muscles she developed were incidental to her main purpose. Vanity was not the primary reason female officers labored in the gym—most endured bodybuilding and weight training for the purpose of safety because someday strength might be called upon to subdue a perpetrator or defend themselves against a stronger opponent. For them, strength could mean the difference between life and death.

Sandy's smile lingered. This woman was toying

with her, and she intended to give it back.

"What's so funny?" Avery asked.

Saying nothing, Sandy applied a bit more pressure to their mutual handshake. Avery's hand involuntarily gave way to Sandy's more powerful grip. A lesser woman might have been humbled, but Avery appeared intrigued. Releasing her hold, Sandy said, "Nice to meet you,

Avery. I see that, like me, you also have a French name, don't you?"

"Yes, I do," Avery answered quickly and then flashed a wide smile with straight white teeth.

"If I remember right," Sandy told her, "Avery means flirtatious." Sandy smiled briefly and then turned away to address Robin. "Listen, Robin, I've got to get going, but I'll check back with you in the morning."

Chapter Twenty-One-: Avery's Thoughts

Thursday, October 14

Although slow, Robin finally caught on to the subtle exchange of interest occurring between the two women. After she closed the front door, she turned to Avery and stared at her.

"What?" Avery asked while running the fingers of her right hand slowly through her shiny black hair.

"You know what."

"Don't worry. I have no intention of seducing Detective What's-her-name."

"The cops call her Lady Persevere."

"Why do they call her that?"

Robin explained the origin of Sandy's nickname, but Avery was barely listening. Her mind was preoccupied with the decision to have sex with this mighty cop whose physical superiority dwarfed her own. There was nothing Avery wanted more than to make the tough detective weak-kneed and vulnerable. What great fun it would be to make all that strength completely useless! Avery grinned to herself, for she intended to have the powerful public servant at her mercy, and she silently predicted that it would not be long in coming.

Detective P's Vulnerability
Friday morning, October 15

As promised, Sandy returned to Robin's the next day to follow up. In response to the doorbell, it was Avery who met her.

"Is Robin here?" Sandy asked.

"No, she isn't," Avery explained. "She said all of this stress and insomnia are turning her into an airhead, so Squeaky and Marie took her to a doctor for some medicine."

"Damn. Okay, just tell her I dropped by. I'll catch her later."

"Should I have her call you at the precinct?" Avery said, then as an afterthought added,

"Detective?"

"No, I'm not officially on duty today."

Avery slightly arched an eyebrow, a movement that did not go unnoticed by Sandy, who suddenly realized the small window of opportunity that Avery had found.

Sandy's mind raced to recall the location of her police radio, which she was happy to note was in her car. Her police radio was noisy and distracting, and on her day off, she was under no obligation to carry it. If this flirtatious woman intended to banter with her, a bunch of annoying radio transmissions would surely spoil the mood.

"Off duty," Avery repeated. "Well then, why don't you come in and visit for a while? We really didn't get a chance to talk yesterday."

"That's because yesterday I was here on official business, not for pleasure."

"I see," said Avery. "Does that mean today you're here for pleasure?"

Sandy wasn't sure how this woman managed to twist her thoughts and words so quickly.

"Actually, what I'm supposed to be working on is a long honey-do list."

Avery cocked her head quizzically. "A honey-do list?"

Sandy nodded.

"I see, and do you receive satisfactory incentives for knocking off a bunch of to-dos for your honey?"

Sandy hesitated, not knowing what Avery was suggesting. But then she took the bait by asking, "Incentives? Such as?"

Avery ran her tongue across her lips. "If honey does, then honey gets," she said suggestively.

Sandy clenched her jaw. It sounded like someone had told this woman about her relationship with Birdie.

"Come on in, Detective," Avery said as she pulled the door wide open and stepped back.

"With all this talk of honey, we don't want to let the flies in."

The boldness of Avery's sexual innuendo was hard to ignore. Personal pride made Sandy want to close the door in this woman's face, but she couldn't deny that she was drawn to such overt flirtatiousness. Against her better judgment, Sandy accepted the invitation and stepped inside.

The truth was that Sandy seldom flirted with women. The impenetrable wall she erected normally helped her resist flirtatious moments. Through misadventures, she was beginning to view sexual experiences as a dangerous path, leading toward commitments that she could not make. But then again, most women were more subtle than Avery. Smiling inwardly, Sandy whispered under her breath, "This woman is unique."

Sandy decided to step inside to satisfy her

curiosity and desire for amusement—nothing more. She did not believe she could be seduced but saw this as an opportunity to let her hair down a little. Sandy pushed away serious thoughts and allowed herself a sense of playfulness. Robin isn't here, and this is my day off. I suppose a little sexual bantering could be fun. So if this woman wants to flirt, bring it on!

Sandy sauntered into the kitchen where Avery offered her coffee. "No thanks, I don't drink coffee."

"Well then, perhaps a protein drink or a thick steak to feed growing muscle?" Avery asked.

"To feed muscle?" Sandy asked. "Oh, does this mean you're still harboring resentment over the fact that my handshake was stronger than yours?" Avery made no effort to answer her question.

Sandy stood at the sink with folded arms, waiting for a response, but Avery didn't give her the satisfaction. Instead, her intense green eyes openly roved Sandy's body. When at last their gazes met, Sandy felt a crack in her calm reserve. Unsettled, she responded by trying to hold tight to her composure.

"At the risk of using an old cliché," Avery said, "I have to say, you are definitely tall, and

I find you handsome, as well."

Sandy felt her face flush. Women often called her tall but never tall and handsome.

"Uh, thanks," she stammered, "quite a compliment, coming from such an attractive woman."

Avery laughed. "Compliments are better when they aren't forced," she said and then delivered a wide grin.

"That wasn't forced!" Sandy protested meekly.

"I didn't mean to put you on the spot," Avery said while her gaze continued roving Sandy's body.

Sandy sensed this last statement was untrue. Avery most certainly did intend to put her on the spot, and she was doing an excellent job of it!

"Could I have your hand?" Avery suddenly asked.

Sandy smiled but didn't unfold her arms. "Now I know you don't want to shake hands again."

"No," Avery agreed. "You're right about that. I was just wondering…have you ever had your palm read?"

"No, I haven't."

Avery stepped forward. "Could I have your hand, please?" she repeated.

Sandy didn't really believe in palm reading nor did she peg Avery as the psychic type, but she shrugged and offered her right hand.

Softly, Avery took her hand in her own, moving closer and bending over Sandy's upturned palm. She appeared to be scrutinizing the lines in Sandy's palm.

"I see a long lifeline," she started.

"Do you mean a long lifeline for a regular person or long for a cop?" Sandy asked.

Again, Avery ignored her question. "In your immediate future, I see a romantic interlude with an attractive female stranger."

Both women laughed. Sandy had not seen that coming! Now she found that Avery, with whom she intended only to banter with, had somehow lured her inside her personal space.

"I understand that you have vowed to be a nun," Avery said softly.

Sandy guessed her expected answer was supposed to be "I'm no nun." But damned if that wasn't Avery's second reference to her relationship with Birdie!

Sandy straightened up, suddenly feeling resentful of this intrusion into her life.

Unaware of the bitterness she had inadvertently fostered, Avery caressed the outside of Sandy's hand, first with the palms of her hands and then with her lips. From there, she progressed to alternating light kisses and gentle licks with her moistened tongue.

Feeling the unexpected warmth of her hand and viewing the sight of Avery's lips and tongue on her skin, Sandy struggled to remain unruffled. She neither withdrew her hand nor made any verbal acknowledgment of Avery's intimate attention. Mind over body.

Sandy's mind raced. Why does a subject as boring as my sex life tend to spread like wildfire? More to the present moment, how could I manage to allow a little harmless flirting to progress so rapidly? It was amazing to Sandy that nothing sexual had occurred in her life for a long time, and now, without warning, things were moving entirely too fast.

Sandy tightened her jaw muscles. What gives Avery the right to refer to my highly personal and intimate relationship with Birdie? The next thing she knew, Sandy was angry. In plain and simple cop language, she considered telling this forward-speaking woman to go fuck herself. However, as Avery's attentive kissing and licking progressively continued up her wrist and onto her forearm, Sandy realized she was leery about mentioning a dangerous word like fuck to a woman such as Avery!

Inside her mind, a debate ensued. The angelic half of Sandy's mind whispered, Pull away, you fool, while her devilish body desperately craved the attention and begged for more. An ache grew deep within her loins.

With valiant concentration, Sandy managed one

last flippant remark. "I don't think this was what I had in mind!"

"How odd," Avery said playfully, "because this is exactly what I had in mind."

Wordlessly, Avery placed Sandy's hand across her right breast and gazed knowingly into conflicted eyes. Both stood in anticipation of what would happen next.

Sex-starved Sandy closed her eyes and sighed deeply. It was decision time. She could run and escape the guilt that always followed such encounters or seize the moment and embrace this rare opportunity.

When she opened her eyes, she did so as a new person. Sandy decided she would indeed seize the moment; however, despite what Avery thought, she was not going to remain in charge. Avery had played her part well, but as far as Sandy was concerned, Avery's reign was over. Only one question remained—Was this woman ready to relinquish control of her body to someone more powerful, to a woman who was willing to pick up where she had left off?

Wrapping her fingers at the base of Avery's hair, Sandy urged her head slightly backward, exposing the soft flesh of Avery's neck, which she kissed while her other hand roved gently over the distinct rise of an eager nipple beneath the soft fabric of her blouse.

Sandy worked her hand down the back of Avery's neck. She stopped when she reached the small of her back. She then used this part of Avery's body to draw her in closer, holding the smaller woman tight enough to imply possession and control. It was a grasp that turned into an enthusiastic mutual embrace. Sandy wrapped strong but gentle arms around Avery's sleek body and melted into her kisses.

As their lips and bodies pressed together, she

marveled at the fact that being in Avery's arms felt so natural and easy. She also realized how very much she wanted and needed to do this. Her body responded like the engine of a train—slow to begin, then gradually warming up, and once in motion, impossible to stop.

Sandy reached her long arms around Avery, slid them across both buns, and rubbed them possessively. She then moved her hand forward, sliding beneath the fabric of Avery's blouse, to rove boldly across a naked breast, while allowing her fingertips the freedom to gently trace Avery's swollen nipples. Avery shuddered with desire, fanning the flames of Sandy's now cocky and assertive behavior. With graceful ease, she lifted Avery up and sat her on the countertop. Sandy then quickly freed the few buttons on Avery's blouse, exposing the supple breasts she knew were waiting for her hungry mouth.

Sandy's lips and mouth moved from one breast to the other and then upward, planting kisses on Avery's neck, until their lips met, and the two women pressed eagerly into each other with firm and probing kisses.

Avery willingly yielded to Sandy's dominance, groaning lightly, something Sandy hoped was a signal indicating a desire for more. All the while, Avery's fingers alternately roamed across Sandy's muscular arms and broad back.

Cupping Avery's rounded buttocks in her strong hands, Sandy pulled Avery across the countertop until their bodies pressed against each other. She then moved back ever so slightly and caressed Avery's crotch. Even through the fabric, Sandy could feel Avery's warmth. Sandy pushed away from Avery and stared down at the sensuous woman on the countertop before her, savoring the moment. In her arms, she had captured an attractive woman who intensely wanted her. This desire, which Avery clearly communicated, felt terrific and did her ego wonders. If I could only pause this moment in time, I would gladly do so to absorb every minute, every exquisite detail, and bask in its warmth. A smile played about Sandy's lips until Avery interrupted her thoughts.

With a confused look on her face, Avery braced herself with both hands on the countertop and breathlessly asked, "What...what are you doing?"

Sandy took advantage of this break to tease her potential lover. In her carefully observant manner, Sandy recognized Avery was at the point of no return, so she felt secure in her ability to tease her without spoiling anything. Pleasantly powerful thoughts coursed through Sandy's mind—thoughts that she would not cut off. Avery wanted, needed, and would look forward to more. Who is in control now? Sandy silently asked Avery with her eyes.

Sandy gave her a devilish grin, clearly savoring the moment and appreciating that another woman intensely wanted her. This was a thought that briefly amused her. Oh, how quickly sex could turn the tables! Now it was Avery's turn to feel the pain of longing if only for an instant. For too long, it was only in Sandy's dreams that she heard a woman cry out for her and beg for more. Such dreams were good, exceptionally good, but they paled in comparison to the excitement of experiencing such an event!

"Stop teasing me and get back over here," Avery demanded.

Sandy paused a moment longer and then stepped forward, closing the gap between them. Slipping between Avery's legs, she pressed their upper bodies together. In her arms, Avery's body felt slight and feminine. The need to take her completely was overwhelming.

Suddenly impatient, Sandy eased her lips away from soft flesh long enough to make her demand. "Tell me which bed is yours!"

"It's the last one on the right," Avery said. She then wrapped her arms around Sandy's neck and allowed Sandy to carry her down the hallway.

Gazing upon the smaller woman in her arms, Sandy considered that she had not actually expected a sexual encounter, a notion she now thought foolish, because Avery was undoubtedly the type of woman who created unexpected opportunities.

Sandy shoved the door closed with her foot and twisted the lock. , . She then lowered her body onto Avery's. Their kisses became passionately possessive as they feverishly probed beneath each other's clothing to fondle restricted areas. The women then hurriedly removed each other's clothing. Avery tugged at Sandy's pants and shirt, impatient to free her taut physique. As Sandy's body became exposed, Avery's green eyes marveled at her broad shoulders, her finely cut arms, and washboard abs. Sandy's exquisite body heightened Avery's arousal until her realm became that of another time and space. Desire engulfed her. Sandy became enveloped inside a cocoon of warmth, softness, sounds, and smells of this woman.

Avery now communicated her interest with her eyes and hands, taking in Sandy's naked body and enjoying its effects. Both women lay naked, flesh against flesh, warmth against warmth, curves meshed into curves. Sandy slowly gyrated against Avery's body and then brought her knee in between her legs. She pressed against Avery's excited wetness while kissing her lips and thrusting her tongue deep inside her hungry mouth.

After a while, Sandy eased herself downward in her journey to the intimate part of Avery's body, a part that throbbed with anticipation and glistened with wetness. Sandy licked where she knew that licking felt best, and judging from the motions and the noises coming from the back of Avery's throat, she performed very well. Continuing to use her tongue to stimulate Avery's clitoris, Sandy patiently awaited the moment when she felt Avery's need for penetration.

Avery's small gasps and vigorous hip motion were the signals Sandy had been waiting for, but she still held back.

"Oh, you are a wicked woman!" Avery said. "You're torturing me!"

In response, Sandy slid two long and graceful fingers deep inside her. She filled Avery inside, then rhythmically moved them in and out, in and out. Strong fingers pushed into Avery's wetness driven deep by an even stronger forearm. With perfect timing, Sandy slid, skated, and penetrated Avery's feminine body. Plunging in her, pulling out of her, reentering her, and withdrawing from her were actions played out repeatedly again until, at last, ecstasy found orgasm.

For Sandy, lovemaking was an exhilarating process of letting go. For once, she was not checking her desire or holding back from doing what she yearned to do. She felt like a bird taking flight from the confines of its cage. When she rested her head on the pillow beside Avery and closed her eyes, unwillingly, she thought of Birdie.

She had given in to temptation, and now she

weighed whether she should confess her actions or keep quiet. There was a part of her that knew she wanted a repeat of this experience with Avery, yet the exploits she had had with other women had clearly demonstrated the danger of women becoming too attached and too possessive. Her goal now was to prevent herself from getting too close. She believed that it was simpler not to have repeat sex with any woman. To her own dismay, such circumstances were causing her to embrace a chauvinistic attitude of love them and leave them. Until now, she hadn't actually applied such a philosophy. Now she found herself wondering, Am I capable of experiencing intimate sex and then walking away?

Surprisingly, the answer was—yes!

Sandy considered that Avery was a woman who was neither naïve nor innocent. She didn't seem to be the type who considered an impromptu fling as a promise of love and commitment. On the other hand, experience had taught Sandy that lesbians had a strong tendency to confuse lust with love, hence the oft-repeated phrase: Lesbians bring a moving van to their second date.

Sandy suddenly felt a need to flee before the subject of intimacy and a future together came up as post-sex pillow talk. However, her intention to leave ended abruptly when Avery rose on her haunches and, in renewed vitality, announced: "Now…it's your turn!"

Sandy reached out to stop her, but not before Avery's fingers discovered her own well-lubricated opening. Helpless to her desires, Sandy lost all semblance of command or control.

Avery's green eyes glistened in the light, and her grin was wide and cat-like.

Chapter Twenty-two: Bella and Salvia

Friday morning, October 15

The next afternoon, Bella hatched a new plan. "Salvia, what other kind of food do you like?"

"I like lots of things. But my favorite is Mexican."

"I can make good enchiladas and smothered burritos. All we would need are a few things from the store."

"Oh, I don't know," Salvia said. "The store's pretty far from here, and the cost of gas up here in the mountains ran me out of money until I get my next unemployment check." She didn't mention she had been receiving her checks by direct deposit because Salvia's goal was to avoid going out in public and to lay low.

"But you don't know for sure how long that will be."

"No, but however long it is, I guess we'll just have to wait."

"You can use my credit card again," Bella offered. "I have lots of plastic."

"Nah, it wouldn't be safe for me to do that," Salvia said. "Matter of fact, I shouldn't have used it the first time."

"It'll be okay as long as you don't go directly to my bank or buy anything too expensive."

"I don't know. What if they use it to try and track me?"

This, of course, was exactly what Bella was hoping

for, but she knew better than to let on. "Well then, don't use it anywhere around here," she suggested. "Just drive a good distance to one
of those money machines, punch in my PIN, and pull out a bunch of cash."

"Yeah, that's an idea," Sal said, "but it still seems risky to me."

"What about a disguise?" Bella offered. Salvia looked up, her interest piqued.

Salvia's Thoughts
Friday morning, October 15

Salvia Singleton didn't know if Bella really believed she was stupid enough to use her credit card a second time, but the fact that Bella hinted at it made her angry enough to lie to her. Yeah, sure, she was dying to put on a disguise, drive to a different town—in the opposite direction from the last one—and use Bella's credit card again. It was insulting to her intelligence for Bella to think she was that naïve. She knew such activity would flag the authorities. She could just picture a bald detective drawing a big fat red circle on a map—a circle that would include the location of her Quonset hut.

As far as Sal was concerned, using the card once was stupid, but to use it twice was unthinkable. It would be bad enough if the law somehow managed to find them on their own, but the thought of her—a kidnapper—helping them track her down was insane. Good God! Salvia wanted to tell Bella that her suggestions were ridiculous and that she was not as naïve as she obviously thought she was. However, she sensed that her objection to her plan would upset

Bella. Being in a generous mood, Salvia figured it would just be easier to go along with the pretense.

Sal dressed in the most butch clothing she owned, then allowed Bella to remake another two- or three-day-old beard on her, and she drove away in the direction that Bella suggested. However, once she was out of sight, she removed the makeup, changed shirts, and headed to familiar territory. Salvia bought groceries with cash at her usual store and came straight back to Bella.

Bella Alone Again
Friday morning, October 15

While Salvia was gone, once again, Bella was alone, shackled to the wall and waiting anxiously. In her loneliness, she conjured up a steady stream of thoughts about Robin. One thing she knew about Robin was that in a crisis, her finest features came shining through. Robin would have immediately called everyone she knew and notified the police as soon as she was able. And in her dealing with the cops, Robin would be relentless.

"I know you would be here if you could," Bella said to the empty space around her. Robin had always been by her side...until now, and this situation was beyond any loving partner's abilities.

The biggest problem was that Salvia was such a cunning abductor that it was unlikely anyone would figure out who took her or where, including the police. Also, since Robin had only seen Salvia once, it was unlikely she would make a connection. For either one of them to predict that Salvia intended to kidnap her was beyond their wildest dreams.

Although Bella was the one who encouraged

Salvia to leave the hut, after Sal was gone, she doubted the wisdom of her suggestion. When alone and shackled to the steel wall, she was on an emotional roller coaster, wavering back and forth from hopefulness to fear for her life. She felt hopeful because of the possibility that someone might see Salvia: Sal might get videotaped or stopped by a cop, or someone might track her purchases. Yet she was also scared as hell because she could not escape her confinement, which meant that if, for some reason, Sal failed to come back or to tell anyone where Bella was located, there was the possibility that Bella could die a slow, cold, and terribly lonely death.

On the other hand, if Saliva were crafty and lucky enough, Bella could become one of those people she had heard about on the news—an unfortunate being under someone's control for years on end before the situation finally became known.

Why me? It didn't seem fair! There was, in fact, nothing fair about it. She had never done anything to deserve something like this. She never flirted with the woman. Her actions were nothing more than gentle kindness. While growing up, she often saw her parents helping strangers in public places and trusting people they didn't know. What she did with Salvia wasn't any different.

Bella's mind returned to the present. When she considered the character of Robin, Salvia, and herself, instinctively, she knew that she was the most calm and sensible of the bunch. They were qualities that came naturally to her. If she was going to get out of this mess and back to Robin, Bella knew that she had to rely on her own inner strength. This, she surmised, was a situation that called for time and patience, and she summoned all that she had.

Chapter Twenty-three: Footwork

Saturday morning, October 16

Lady Persevere sat across from Detective Spears, noting his mounting frustration with the case.

"Who ever heard of someone getting their sticky paws on someone else's credit card and then only using it once?" he asked.

Sandy knew that in Spears's mind, greed was the driving force for most people, and certainly greed was what Spears was counting on. "Why the devil isn't the card being used again?"

Sandy didn't answer him because she believed there was an entirely different motivating factor in play, but she sensed that Spears didn't want to hear any of her ideas.

While searching the blue Jeeps, Sandy found one owned by a butch-looking woman whose picture resembled the "man" they thought they saw in the video. The first time she visited her address, no one was home, but she would be back.

⁂

Sandy left the office and returned to Salvia's home, where she was delighted to find a bag of trash sitting on the curb in front of her house. Trash was anyone's treasure, and she knew that discarded business papers could be a wealth of information. In a matter of minutes, she found the name of Salvia's old employer.

On her visit to the auto parts store, Sandy was fascinated to learn that the people there had two distinctly different opinions about the same woman.

While wiping his nostril with an index finger, Salvia's former boss claimed that Salvia's recent job performance was not up to par and that he was forced to let her go.

However, Salvia's coworkers raved about her job performance and were vocally upset about her losing her job. They complained about the boss's son, and every one of them stated that Salvia did a hell of a lot better job than he did.

When asked about Salvia's personal life, they clammed up. Sandy surmised that they knew she was a lesbian, and protectively, they refused to talk about it.

Among her fellow detectives and police officers, Sandy sensed that her closest coworkers also knew that she was in a lesbian relationship without being told. She was sure they made frequent guesses about her personal relationship with Birdie. With a degree of envy, Sandy wondered if her own coworkers would be as closed-mouthed and protective as Salvia's.

Through the process of gathering information, going back, uncovering a person's history, and then putting the pieces together, Sandy learned of the hardships that Salvia had endured in the last month. Her mother had died, she lost her job, and the house had caught on fire. Each one of the events was enough stress to unnerve most people. However, given the combination of all three disasters, Sandy knew that for Salvia, stress may have piled up to form a dangerous combination.

In the meantime, Randy Spears was eagerly waiting for the next use of Isabella Sanchez's credit card. Unless Salvia's card was stolen, Spears claimed this was a definite link to the last person who knew of Ms. Sanchez's whereabouts. As for the rest of his team, he believed that Sandy was off on a wild goose chase, desperately looking for the Jeep of "some poor schmuck who probably had nothing more to do with Ms. Isabella Sanchez than the love of the same coffee shop."

However, Sandy was closer to the truth. Operating from the hunch that one lesbian might run off with or be abducted by another, Sandy obtained a photograph of Salvia from the motor vehicle department and showed it to Robin.

"Do you know, or have you ever seen this woman?"

"No...uh, wait a minute," Robin said. "I think I have seen her. Yes, I saw her once." "Where?"

"One of my patients, maybe. No, um, let's see... Oh, I know! I saw her in the waiting room at the emergency room. She was staring at Bella. She was just sitting there staring so intently that it unnerved me."

After five years as a detective, certain words that came from the victims or their loved ones sounded all too familiar. It was common for a victim to report that someone had been lurking around and staring at them and that this behavior had made them feel uneasy. Belatedly, victims often discovered that their gut instincts were dead on.

Sandy felt increasingly certain that she had the right woman. But the frustrating part of it all was that patient confidentiality rules would keep her from reviewing Salvia's emergency room medical record. And she couldn't go to a judge and ask for a subpoena because Salvia had been staring at Bella. So Sandy decided to take Salvia's photograph to her eyewitness from Starbucks.

Unfortunately, this woman previously thought she had seen a man, and even though she conceded that the woman in the photo bore a close resemblance to the man she remembered, she wasn't willing to admit to such a fundamental mistake.

Chapter Twenty-four: Robin Gets Testy

Saturday, October 15

Robin eyed the pizza that Squeaky and Marie brought in. It had pepperoni and black olives and a golden-brown crust, and it smelled wonderful. She watched quietly as Sandy took a giant bite out of her slice.

Trying not to look, Robin stirred her oatmeal with a spoon and felt guilty for her dishonesty. She wouldn't tell these women her thoughts on their food choice because it would do no good. Being truthful in this case would only serve to make them all feel guilty.

Her truth was, there were certain types of food that Robin considered party food. Pizza, popcorn, cake, and pie all fell into this special category, and they were choices that she reserved for special occasions. She thought of these items as celebration food. Ever since Bella's disappearance, Robin had nothing to celebrate. She neither ordered nor intended to eat any of their pizza. When the food arrived and she smelled the aroma of freshly baked crust and melted cheese, her stomach growled. Now as she sat stirring her bland oatmeal, their pizza was an annoying temptation.

Shoving her oatmeal aside, Robin suddenly strode over to the kitchen window, stared outside, and expressed one of the thoughts rattling around in her mind. "Okay," Robin said to everyone present. "I can see how Bella might've been abducted by a man because most men can overpower most women, but how could this happen with a woman? I mean, even if this stranger were more powerful than her, Bella still could put up a decent fight or make noise. At the very least, she could attract attention!"

The noise level in the room suddenly ceased.

"Be careful," Squeaky advised. "You don't want to sound like you're blaming the victim.

None of us really knows what went on. We weren't there."

Robin contemplated her advice for a moment and then asked, "Do you think she seduced her?"

"No," Marie said. "Bella was never interested in other women, even on the nights when you were working, and we all went out together."

Robin pictured in her mind how Bella had ignored the woman in the waiting room.

Sandy stepped forward. "Most people, who are not really powerful—and this includes some men, as well as women—tend to use tricks or gimmicks." "Like what?" Robin asked.

"Well," Sandy stalled, as the tactics of serial murderer Ted Bundy came to her mind. Silently, Sandy recalled how Ted Bundy used a cast on his arm for sympathy and then asked victims for help carrying objects to his car. When they reached the car, he struck them on the head with a hammer. However, Sandy certainly didn't want to mention the tactics of a cold-blooded serial killer as an example.

"Um, you know, like showing off a puppy for example," she said quickly.

"Hmm," Robin said. "I guess that would work. Bella's a real sucker for animals."

Bella Bides Her Time
Saturday, October 15

Salvia returned to the Quonset hut without incident, and the two women spent a communicative day together. Outside of biding her time and keeping Salvia calm, there was little else that Bella could do. However, it was a situation that frustrated the devil out of her. Another day had passed, and no one found her, which prompted her to start thinking up schemes to get Salvia to go to the store again.

"Salvia, I started my period. Do you have any tampons?" she asked.

"The pads are in the corner, by the toilet," Sal said.

"Pads?" she asked, pretending she had never seen them.

"Yep."

"I can't stand pads," Bella whined. "Don't you have any tampons?"

"No."

"Oh, man. Really?"

Salvia ignored her last question.

"How about something for cramps, like Midol?" she asked.

"No," Sal said with a degree of annoyance.

"Well, what do you have?" Bella asked.

"Aspirin."

"Aspirin gives me a stomachache," she said while making a face.

Salvia sighed, hesitated, and then she said, "Okay, I can go get you whatever you want." Bella smiled to herself. There was hope, and it could be right around the corner.

Chapter Twenty-five: Taking Matters in Her Own Hands

Sunday, October 16

Robin was sick and tired of feeling useless and waiting around for nothing. She felt certain that Salvia was the one who kidnapped Bella, and she didn't want to wait around for the police to collect enough evidence so they could finally get a search warrant. Although the police had to concern themselves with legalities and technicalities and the security of their jobs, Robin only had two concerns—Bella and the fact that time was running out.

The hands of justice were so bound up with red tape that it was going to take too much time for the police to find out all they needed to know about Salvia Singleton. To a certain extent, Robin understood their position. These officers had the watchful eye of the public on them. Careers were on the line. They didn't really have a choice, they had to play by the rules, but she didn't, and no one was watching her!

Utilizing the internet, she found Salvia Singleton's address. In broad daylight, she parked her truck in front of the fire-damaged house, and then she started sweating bullets because the next step of her plan was to break in.

Robin looked down at the burglar tools she had placed on her floor mat. She heard a rumor that there was a technique where you slip a key into a door lock, then tap it with a hammer, which would cause the lock to pop open. She liked the idea because, if it worked, there would be no visible damage to the house. However, she had no clue if it really worked.

Besides bringing a handful of keys and a hammer, she also brought a large screwdriver and a sturdy crowbar. Robin vowed that if she discovered Salvia or Bella inside, she would play it safe and call the cops, but if there was no one home, she would go in, no matter what the consequences.

She had not mentally prepared herself for any other options. However, when she pulled up in front of Salvia's house, she noticed a charred and melted television set by the curb, a propped open front door, and workers trudging in and out. It looked to her like this homeowner had experienced a small fire.

The idea of a fire worried her at first, but then she sensed that Bella was not there. As for getting inside the house, she knew workers, particularly male workers, well enough to know that such guys tended to be lax about security and were rarely suspicious of women. She also knew, from working at the hospital, that the more arrogant and self-assured a person acted, the less likely anyone was to question their presence. She turned away from the burglar tools because she now realized she could stroll right through the front door and just pretend she belonged there.

"Hi guys," she said in a cheerful tone of voice. "Salvia sent me to pick up some insurance papers and things."

"Hello" and "okay" is all they said before turning their attention back to their jobs.

Robin didn't know exactly what she was looking

for, but she assumed that a diary, notations, tax records, or proof of ownership of a second property would tell her what she needed to know.

Throwing Darts

Sunday, October 16

After seeing Salvia's picture, Detective Spears begrudgingly admitted that she did bear a resemblance to the person who used the credit card. But they were then frustrated by the fact that Salvia could not be found.

Down the hallway from Spears's office, Lady Persevere began a common routine she used when she felt stuck—she threw darts at a dartboard in her office. She claimed that throwing a sharp point at a specific target helped to ease her frustration level and rechanneled her thinking. The third dart she threw took a bad bounce, veered away from the wall, and landed on her bookshelf. It came to rest on top of a book titled The Battered Woman. While studying abusive men, the author noted a tendency to live in isolated areas such as the foothills outside of Denver. According to the author, isolation was an intentional means of depriving victims of a support system.

"Isolation, cabins…that's it! What if they own a second property?" Sandy said aloud. She yanked out her chair and glared eagerly at her computer screen. "Tax records are public records."

Sandy searched for property under the name of Salvia's mother. A property did turn up, but it was listed as unimproved. A garage-type structure was on the land, but there were no utilities or houses, but that wasn't enough to deter her. In Sandy's mind, if any type of building existed, Salvia and her Jeep could be there, which meant it had to be checked out because Bella could be there, too...dead or alive. "Alive, I hope!" Sandy shouted as she shoved back her chair and scribbled the address on a scrap of paper.

Silently, she savored the notion that the best part was yet to come—when she informed Detective Spears that she discovered a mountain property owned by Salvia's mother and located within forty miles of where the person who resembled Salvia had last used the credit card.

Raymond Spears listened to her findings and was at once willing to check it out. He offered her a ride, but Sandy politely refused, preferring instead to follow him in her own vehicle.

Using maps, Detective Spears led the way. Sandy followed in happy solitude, with her mind in high gear. Wild goose chases were common for detectives, but for the sake of "Mister Impatience," she hoped this wouldn't be one. Regardless, this was a lead worth following. Whether the mountain garage was legally livable space or not, there was a very real possibility that Salvia could be using her mother's building to hold Bella Sanchez prisoner. In that case, all sorts of scenarios could greet them when they arrived. They might surprise Salvia, or they might be fired upon. There was the possibility they could find and free Bella in good condition, but also the possibility that they could discover her dead body.

As they drew nearer, Detective Spears also shared her anxiety because she noticed that he didn't slow, even when the road turned to gravel, and they had to swerve around sharp turns. Choking on the dust that Spears's vehicle kicked up, Sandy raced to roll up her window. Through a mixture of pine and aspen trees, no buildings of any sort were initially visible, but that was common in the mountains owing to uneven terrain and plentiful evergreen trees. Cabins were often nestled into hillsides and difficult to spot until a person was upon them. Besides, all the dust the lead vehicle churned up compromised Sandy's vision. Suddenly, Spears swerved to one side of the narrow road, and he braked so hard that she nearly crashed into him.

"Dumbass!" she muttered.

Spears motioned with his left arm for her to pull up alongside. Sandy backed up a little, then eased her SUV within inches of his car. With little space between trees on both sides, she recognized his plan was to block any vehicle trying to leave the area.

Detective Spears opened the trunk of his vehicle, handed her a set of binoculars, then yanked out a high-powered rifle for himself.

"It's just over the next rise," he whispered, "to the left."

The detectives climbed the hill in silence. Once they crested the hill, they took positions behind trees and studied the building. The fact that it was larger than Sandy imagined was promising, but no vehicle was in sight.

Quietly, the detectives circled the building. Light smoke was coming from a round metal vent that exited high up on one end of the building. That was an encouraging sign. Working as a well-trained unit, they sneaked to the back side of the hut, just below a window on the west side.

"If I lift you up, do you think you could see in

that window?" Spears whispered.

For a moment, Sandy nearly laughed. She dwarfed the height of one-quarter of her male cohorts. She was a solid woman and almost bigger than Spears. Lifting her would be no easy task. However, she nodded obediently, put a foot into his laced hands, and rose toward the window. Grasping the cold metal ridges of the building with her hands, she tried to lift as much of her weight off Spears as she could.

At first, she could barely see inside. She scrambled farther up the side of the metal hut and onto Detective Spears's shoulders, then struggled to keep herself as still as possible. The first thing she saw was that the interior was not being used as a storage facility or garage; instead, someone had arranged it like a house. Sandy's heart raced. Cupping her hands over the window to block the glare of the afternoon sun, she scanned the room. She thought she saw movement near a wall. Yes, a foot! There was a foot, and it was moving! She motioned for Spears to put her down. As she whispered what she had seen, she was happy to share the excitement that registered on Raymond Spears's face.

They scanned the horizon for signs of vehicles, then stole cautiously around toward the front of the building. At the corner, Spears laid down his rifle, pulled his handgun from its holster, and then held up his other hand.

"Cover me!" he whispered as he made his way toward the door.

Sandy pulled her weapon and went into high alert mode. But as soon as Spears discovered that the solid steel door was locked, he quickly returned.

"What if we take a position on each side of the

door and call out to them?" she suggested.

"Okay," he agreed, "go ahead." And they slipped into position.

Sandy drew in her breath, and then using her loudest voice, she shouted, "This is the police! We have you surrounded. Come out with your hands up!"

"Help!"

Frozen in place, the detectives raised an eyebrow at each other. The call for help was faint, but they both heard it.

"Help! I'm in here!" a distinctively female voice yelled.

Keeping his body close to the side of the building, Spears banged on the steel door with his nightstick, then drew his arm back and waited, making sure to keep his body well off to one side.

"This is the police," Spears shouted, "how many people are in there?" "No one," Bella called out. "I mean, just me!" "Come to the door!" Spears instructed.

"I can't! I'm handcuffed to the wall!" Bella said.

Not only would it be loud, but it would also be dangerous to shoot at a padlock on a metal building when there was a concrete footing beneath it. Instead, Spears instructed Sandy to keep a lookout behind him as he pulled small locksmith tools from the side pocket of his camouflage pants. He knelt on the gravel just outside the door. From there, he began the tedious task of threading tiny lock-picking tools into the keyhole and trying to turn tumblers that would cause the cheap lock to open. Meanwhile, Sandy kept a careful watch to prevent an ambush by Salvia if she happened to return.

At last, the tumblers responded, and the detectives opened the door. But they did so fully armed, and they entered by the book.

They did a quick once-over of the interior, but they did not immediately spot their victim. They saw an empty bed closer to them, but then, on the far side close to the floor, they saw Bella huddled near the exterior steel wall.

"Are you Isabella Sanchez?" Sandy asked gently. "Yes!"

With the adrenaline rush of having found their hostage, Sandy noted that Detective Spears became pumped up. Even though Bella was in tears and handcuffed to a wall, Spears raced over and practically jumped on her. Deliberately stepping in front of him, Sandy touched

Bella gently and spoke to her calmly. "It's okay, it's all over. We're going to take you home."

But Spears didn't take her cue and would not be put off. As Sandy was fishing out her handcuff key to unlock the cuffs, Spears began shouting at Bella. "Who did this to you? Was it Salvia Singleton?" "Yes," Bella whimpered.

"Well, don't you worry, miss, because we're gonna catch her and send her butt straight to prison! Kidnapping is a federal offense! She'll be locked up for a good long time! Do you know where she went? How long has she been gone?"

Sandy noticed that Bella flinched when Detective Spears was making what he thought were reassuring comments about what he planned to do with Salvia once they caught up with her.

"Hey, Detective, could you tone it down a little?" she asked him.

But he deliberately ignored her because Raymond Spears had become like a bloodhound on a fresh trail. In his single-minded pursuit of the bad guy, Spears undoubtedly felt justified in riding this adrenaline rush to the very end. His face reddened, and beads of perspiration dotted his forehead.

"When did she leave?" he asked.

"Maybe about an hour ago," Bella said quietly.

"Where did she go?" he demanded.

Bella hesitated.

"I said, where did she go?" he repeated impatiently.

Sandy was about to stop him again when Bella said, "To some little town about forty miles west of here, the same place where she used my credit card."

That was enough to get Spears ready for takeoff. "Take care of the victim," he barked, and he was gone.

There were times that Sandy was embarrassed that she was part of the police force, and this was one of them. It was obvious that Spears was far more concerned about crediting himself with a capture than he was with comforting a victim. She noticed Bella silently watching him leave.

The instant he was gone, Sandy apologized for his behavior. "I'm sorry he talked like that to you, he's just all fired up," she said. "Are you okay? Did she hurt you?"

"No...she just wanted...she's just mixed up!" Bella said. "She doesn't deserve..." And then she cut herself short.

At that moment, Sandy knew that Bella had intentionally sent Detective Spears in the wrong direction. Sandy unlocked the cuffs and helped Bella to a chair in the kitchen.

She withdrew her cellphone and smiled brightly. "I know someone who would love to talk to you," she said with a wide grin. With that, she handed Bella her phone. But Bella fumbled with the small and slippery gadget. Her fingers were shaking so hard that Sandy gently took her phone back and dialed the number for her.

"Hello?" Robin answered uncertainly.

"Baby, it's me!" Bella said.

"Bell? Bella? Are you all right?"

"Yes, honey, I'm okay! The police found me!"

"Oh! Thank God, thank God! I thought…I was so afraid…I didn't know," she said with a voice that was cracking. "I was scared I might never see you again! Oh, honey, I missed you so much! Where are you?"

"I don't know," Bella said, turning to Sandy. "Where am I?"

"Tell her that we're in Salvia's mother's Quonset hut in the mountains."

"I heard that," Robin said. "I'm about halfway there already."

"What? What do you mean halfway here? How could that be?"

"I went into Salvia's house and looked it up. I figured if the police couldn't find you, then, honey, you'd better believe I would! I'll be there soon!"

"I didn't hear that," Sandy muttered.

Sandy waited patiently for the tearful phone call to end, and then she eased her way into teasing out the truth. "Listen, Bella, things don't have to go the way that Detective Spears made out. You see, a person like Salvia, who has had so many major losses in her life… losses that all piled up on her at the same time…well, a person like that is seen as a tragic figure. There is such a thing as temporary insanity. It's utilized by people who have always been responsible citizens but fell off the edge during or after a tragedy. Experts like to use it for people who, with professional help, are likely to go back to leading quiet law-abiding lives again. And if anyone fits into that category, it seems to me that Salvia Singleton does. A person like Salvia doesn't belong in a federal penitentiary, she belongs in a mental health facility where she can get help." The expression on Bella's face was a mixture of confusion and guilt. This encouraged Sandy, so she prepared to continue. She paused and noticed Bella bite her upper lip.

"Listen," Sandy continued, "I don't know what she told you, but Salvia had it rough with her mother. The woman wasn't right. Salvia didn't deserve to lose her job, either. Her boss was an asshole. And then, with the house fire and everything, it was probably all just too much for her."

Bella still said nothing.

"But I'm not saying what she did to you was right, far from it. Salvia took a part of your life away, and she scared the hell out of a whole lot of people. Bella, what I'm trying to say is that you sort of have an obligation to make sure that Salvia doesn't get away and do this sort of thing to someone else. What she did was dangerous. You don't want her to make a mistake and accidentally kill someone, do you?" Bella lowered her head.

Sensing she was getting through to Bella, Sandy continued. "Salvia really does need some professional help, and this way, she won't be able to refuse it." Sandy briefly waited and then said with gentle insistence, "I know that you know this." "Yeah," Bella said quietly.

"Also, I think you know where Salvia is, and correct me if I'm wrong, but she isn't in the direction that you sent Detective Spears." Bella's lips broke into a sly smile.

"Did Salvia tell you where she was going?" Sandy asked gently.

"No, she lies to me about it," Bella said.

"Then what makes you so sure she didn't go the same way that you sent Detective Spears?"

"Because I saw the last receipt from the store," Bella said. "Salvia just goes along with me. She pretends to go where I suggest and pretends to use my credit card, but she doesn't really go there. She's too smart for that. She went to a small town called Pine Ridge, and she's using cash that I think she may have gotten from an insurance check."

"Okay," Sandy said, "let's get you back to the main road so Robin can find us."

The two women walked around to the back side of the hut and scrambled up the rocky ridge, which was the fastest route to Sandy's waiting vehicle. Once inside the SUV, she smiled at Bella and gently rubbed her shoulder with the palm of her right hand, relieved that things had turned out so well and that Bella's ordeal was finally over. Sandy was guiding her SUV down the sloping gravel road when, without warning, Saliva Singleton's royal blue Jeep suddenly loomed into view.

"Duck!" Sandy shouted as she shoved Bella below the level of the dashboard.

Then, pretending to be alone and to act like any normal gravel road driver, Sandy eased her vehicle downhill to the edge of the dirt road and politely waved for Salvia to pass.

As the vehicles drew even, the two drivers exchanged glances. Salvia continued only a short distance past them and then drew her Jeep to a halt.

Realizing that Salvia was on to her, Sandy threw

her SUV into reverse and backed up just far enough on the dirt road to successfully block the Jeep from escaping onto the main road. Then she jumped out and with one hand around the grip of her pistol, she eased toward the back of Salvia's idling Jeep. When the door of the Jeep sprang open, Sandy drew her gun.

"Halt! Police! Stay where you are!"

But Salvia didn't follow orders. She took off, racing up the sloping mountain, as she dodged and weaved her way between pine trees.

Even though Sandy believed her location was too remote for immediate help, she grabbed her radio with her left hand and shouted for backup.

Meanwhile, Salvia disappeared into the trees.

Sandy ran back to Bella's door. "Does she have a gun?" she shouted.

"What?"

"Does she have a gun?" Sandy repeated.

"I never saw one," Bella answered.

"Stay there!" she commanded, then sprinted after her suspect.

Sandy didn't know what to expect when she crested the small hill and peered through the trees. It occurred to her that there were multiple trees and small boulders for a person to hide behind and that it was possible she may have lost the woman. To her surprise, just ahead, she easily spotted Salvia in a blue flannel shirt racing up the hill. Sandy took into consideration the tricky footing on this lightly traveled path. Pine needles on top of loose rock were making footing unstable, along with patches of snow, but she noticed that Sal didn't falter. She knows where she's going. Sandy broke into long, careful strides.

They were both making steady progress up the

mountainside when Salvia suddenly drew to a complete stop. Grasping on to the long needles of a pine tree, Sal drew heavy breaths and looked about uncertainly. Sandy stopped to assess the situation. She saw no weapon on her fugitive. Tentatively, Sandy moved forward, and as she did so, she climbed the rise of the hillside just enough so that the terrain below Salvia's stopping point was clearly visible. The desperate woman had reached the edge of a cliff and was eyeing the drop-off that loomed before her.

"Whoa," Sandy said gently.

"Stop!" Sal said as she struggled to catch her breath. "Stop or I'll jump!"

"Okay," Sandy agreed. "No problem. See? I've stopped. Now let's just take a minute here and calm down."

"Calm down?" Salvia asked. "Calm down?" she shouted.

"Yeah." Sandy leaned against the side of a large pine tree to appear calm and nonthreatening. She felt the palm of her gun hand press into a gooey blob of pine sap but made a conscious effort to ignore it.

"Just take a few minutes…catch your breath… and we'll talk about this," Sandy instructed.

"No!" Salvia shot back. "It's too late to talk!"

"It's never too late to talk. Remember, Salvia, no one has gotten hurt, so it's not too late.

Besides, I'm here…you're here…and I'm listening."

"Oh, bullshit!" Saliva shouted vehemently. "This is just a game you're playing, something they teach you all in cop school. They teach you how to pretend like you give a shit, just so you can slap handcuffs on a live person instead of scraping up a dead one."

"Salvia, I'm not just any cop, you know. You were on the baseball team, so you probably know that I'm Marie's cousin," she calmly said.

"No shit?" Sal asked slowly. "You mean, you're the famous lesbian detective?" "Not famous but definitely lesbian," Sandy said modestly.

"Well, I'm sorry to cut you out of your arrest quota," Salvia said, "but there's somewhere else I'd rather go than prison."

"Just do me one favor," Sandy said. "Talk to me a little bit first. Would you at least do that for me?"

"Why? So that you can stall long enough for your back-up to arrive?"

"You have plenty of time," Sandy said. "No one is anywhere close. We're in the middle of nowhere."

"What do you mean nowhere? Why, we're right next to the famous Baby Doe condo," Salvia said with a sneer.

"Baby Doe?" Sandy asked.

"Never mind," Salvia said. "That's just a poor person's joke."

"Look, I understand that you've been through an awful lot of crap lately—" "Ha! You have no idea!" Salvia shouted.

"Well, no...not about all of it. But I know you lost your mom, and I know about the fire and how you lost your job, and I know that none of this was your fault."

Salvia turned to face Sandy, then stared at her. Minutes seemed to crawl by as the women quietly faced each other.

Sandy's mind raced. She considered various comments to make, but in a situation like this, it was dangerous to blurt anything out without careful forethought. She knew very well that the main point of suicide negotiation was to get the victim to talk.

Salvia's obvious shock that Sandy knew so much about her had clearly registered on her face. Hopefully, that thought would be followed by one where she came to realize that someone cared about her.

The next goal should be to give her a reason to live.

Sandy tried to get into Sal's mind. Salvia was probably thinking it was just part of the job to try to save her. Nothing more.

"I really don't have much to live for," Sal said quietly, "and I don't want to go to prison, so I'll see you later, Detective." With those words, Salvia released her grip on the pine tree and turned to face the cliff before her.

"Salvia, wait!" a chorus of two women's voices yelled at the same time.

Salvia and Sandy turned to see Bella hurrying up the trail.

Bella's dark gaze locked on to Salvia's red-rimmed blue eyes, and neither woman moved. Salvia was like a deer frozen in headlights. She looked wide-eyed, frightened, and clearly uncertain of her next move. Since there was an undeniable connection between the two women, Sandy realized that Bella would have a better chance of talking her off the ledge than she would. If Sandy could have made herself invisible at that moment, she gladly would have done so.

Bella put both hands out in front of her, as if reaching out to Saliva to bridge the distance between them.

Salvia looked from one woman to the other, then her gaze again settled on Bella. As she watched the two women, Sandy's mind was racing. Although Salvia may have thought it was her job as a police officer to try to save her, Sal knew for sure that it was not Bella's job. Depending on what she had done to her, Salvia might jump to the conclusion that Bella wanted her dead. But Sandy was reading signs in this situation that said otherwise; Bella's voluntary presence, the look in her eyes, and her pleading voice, these were unmistakable signs of caring.

"Salvia, please don't do this." Bella's dark eyes were like liquid pools and her voice sincere.

No one moved for two or three long minutes. The air smelled of pine trees, and the women's features were unevenly cast in stripes of sunshine that shone between the trees. Then Salvia took one last look at the base of the shallow cliff before her, and with gravel crunching beneath her feet, she slowly turned away from the cliff. She took one step toward them with her shoulders sagging like the defeated and the defenseless. She then stared dejectedly at the ground.

Sandy considered what might be running through Salvia's mind. Maybe anger because of the way that things turned out. Possibly defeat that she lost her human treasure. And now shame for having been caught.

"I'm sorry, Bella. I'm sorry I kidnapped you. I just lost my head," Salvia said.

"I'm okay, Salvia," Bella responded. "You didn't hurt me. In fact, we kind of got to know each other."

"Yeah, well, now you can go back to Robin."

Bella stopped breathing for a moment. Everyone knew Bella was going back to Robin, so Sandy figured maybe Robin was not a safe topic.

"But, Salvia," Bella said slowly, "there's nothing

that says that you and I can't be friends."

"Oh, sure, I'll bet Robin would be thrilled to death with that idea!" Salvia said, but her face softened.

Planting the idea of a continued friendship would undoubtedly give Salvia hope. Sandy appreciated Bella's kind and forgiving nature, especially after everything Salvia had put her through. An ordinary victim would have stayed in the Jeep. In fact, Sandy had ordered her to stay put. Surely, Salvia realized no one made Bella get out and come offer a hand of friendship to her. She had done this of her own free will. An opportunity to keep Bella in her life and the desire to reach up out of her darkness must have finally overwhelmed Salvia's desperate plan to bring her life to an end.

Salvia looked again toward the cliff. Sandy was wondering if Salvia felt there was no graceful way out.

"We can get you some help," Bella offered.

"Help?" Salvia asked. "You mean, like a loony bin? What makes you think I want to go to a loony bin?"

"Well," Bella said, then hesitated, "I don't know about you, but I always wanted to learn how to weave baskets!" Then a broad and dimpled grin spread across Bella's gentle face.

Her unexpected words took Salvia by surprise; it broke the ice and made the desperate woman smile.

Sandy continued to stand very still, hardly daring to breathe. Whatever happened between these two obviously served to form some kind of positive connection.

"Come on," Bella ventured. "Don't go acting like a man…getting lost in life and refusing to ask for help. Be brave. Let other people help you."

Salvia stared at Bella and Sandy. "Okay," she

finally said.

Sandy was glad she had no fight on her hands with Salvia. That was how she preferred it. After she put Salvia safely away in her SUV, Sandy flagged down Robin's truck as it came bouncing and winding its way up the narrow gravel road.

Robin leaped from the vehicle, and Sandy watched with pleasure as Bella rushed into Robin's protective arms. The two women desperately clung to each other, crying, smiling, and hugging. They wrapped their arms around each other and held on tight, like two people who feared the thought of ever letting go again.

Sandy did her duty by radioing others, and then she pulled her well-worn copy of Miranda rights from her pocket and began the familiar words without looking at the card.

"Salvia," she began, "you have the right to remain silent. Anything you say can and will be used against you in a court of law. You have the right to an attorney. If you cannot afford an attorney, one will be provided for you. If you decide to answer questions now without an attorney present, you will still have the right to stop answering at any time until you talk to an attorney. Do you understand these rights as I have read them to you?"

"Yes," Salvia said. There was a silence and then Salvia said dryly, "I see you're back to being a cop."

Sandy looked into Salvia's eyes. "I never stopped being a cop, but many of us cops also try to be human."

Sandy drove far more cautiously out of the area than she had on the way in. At last, she turned onto smooth asphalt and cruised slowly down the mountain. No longer was she experiencing an adrenaline rush from approaching the unknown. She knew the county jail they were headed for very well, and she was not fond of it. It was a noisy place with angry and dispirited people. For that reason, Sandy was sorry it would be Salvia's first placement.

The steering wheel began to vibrate, then it pulled hard to the right. Sandy let off the accelerator, guided her vehicle safely onto the edge of the asphalt, and got out to inspect it. The right front tire was so flat that the vehicle leaned to the right. Sandy had two choices— she could call for help or change it herself. A flat tire was no big deal, but Salvia's presence complicated things. It was too dangerous to jack a vehicle up with a person inside. Salvia would have to come out. Sandy then thought to check the condition of the spare tire. She pressed hard into the rubber and found there was too much give; the spare was low on air. It was time to call a tow truck for herself and a black and white to transport Salvia to jail.

Chapter Twenty-six: Salvia's Thoughts

Sunday, October 17

Sandy removed her cuffs, and the responding female officer clapped her own pair of cuffs onto Salvia with an efficient flip of the wrist. This officer cuffed Salvia's hands behind her back, which was far more uncomfortable. Salvia heard the metal ratcheting as the officer squeezed the cuffs closed tighter than necessary. Salvia was a powerfully built and stocky woman whose arms were not as flexible as this woman obviously thought they were. The cold metal bands bit uncomfortably into the sensitive bones of her inner wrists.

"They hurt," Salvia complained. "You have them too tight."

The officer took off her sunglasses and stared directly into Salvia's eyes. As their faces drew even, she glared at Salvia and, in an edgy voice, said, "I hope you aren't planning on causing me any problems."

"No, ma'am," Salvia said quickly.

The backseat of the police cruiser was made of plastic. It was hard, cold, and unforgiving. As Salvia sat with her hands cuffed behind her back, she realized the officer intended to leave her like that—in a position where she could neither wipe her eyes, blow her nose, or scratch her face. She looked at the floor and noticed a type of fastener that undoubtedly served the purpose of anchoring handcuffs.

"Excuse me, ma'am, but could you cuff me to the

floor instead of leaving my hands behind my back?"

"Nope…standard operating procedure," the officer said.

Salvia didn't believe her. She noticed there was no seat belt. If they got in a wreck, Salvia would fly face first into an iron grid divider. For Salvia, the next forty minutes were long and uncomfortable.

When they arrived at the county jail, the officer announced this on her radio, and in response, a wide metal garage door opened. The officer pulled the car inside but didn't open Salvia's car door until the garage door closed completely.

"Probably more standard operating procedure," Salvia muttered to herself. Two male officers leaned against the doorway. In Salvia's mind, the roomy garage was a human "trap" where feisty prisoners could be yanked from a car while multiple officers ran out and beat the crap out of them with their hands cuffed behind their back. Salvia guessed her theory about this was right, too, when the two men caught sight of her—a cooperative female prisoner—and their young male faces clearly registered disappointment.

She was obviously nothing to them, not the excitement of trouble, not the intrigue of sexual attraction. She was simply…nothing.

Salvia expected the first thing they would do was fingerprint and photograph her, just as she had seen on television, but instead, a deputy asked her to step into a small concrete room, then the minute she entered, a solid metal door was closed behind her.

"May I have my phone call?" Salvia shouted through the edge of the massive door.

"I've got some things to do," the chunky female jailer said to the air in front of her as she walked away in the opposite direction. "I'll be back later…" Her voice trailed off as she continued down the cinder block hallway. Looking out the tiny glass door, Sal watched her jailer disappear. Sal realized she was now a prisoner who didn't even merit the decency of someone looking at her when they spoke.

Salvia examined the room. There was a small shower area and a one-piece toilet. Tiny bits of paper littered the floor, and the room smelled like urine. Since she knew that jails used the free labor of prisoners, in her mind, there was no excuse for it to be so dirty. Minutes ticked slowly by. Then came the conversations of male officers joking with Salvia's jailer, the one who claimed she had "things to do."

"The next thing you know that puke bucket will be waving his dick around like a fucking flag," a male voice said.

"Yeah," the jailer agreed, "but that bitch is even worse. Even when you compare her to that fucking prick that she came in with, she's still an asshole of the highest order."

Salvia shook her head. Why would a jailer adopt the same gutter language as some of their inmates? It seemed to Sal that these female jailers were too foul-mouthed to be attractive to men and too insensitive to be attractive to women.

Although Salvia liked women, including butch women, which half of the jailers probably were, she didn't find any of these women the least bit attractive owing to their attitudes. Perhaps Detective P was the only one. It occurred to Salvia that if that was the case, she hoped to God the kind detective stayed the hell away from rubbing elbows with this hellhole of inhumanity.

Chapter Twenty-seven: Party time

Sunday night, October 17

After Sandy's tire was changed and the paperwork done, she headed for the party at Robin and Bella's house, hoping to be re-energized. She was not disappointed; the place was rocking! Large outdoor speakers were blaring the song Celebration by Kool and the Gang. As Sandy came through the gate into the backyard, someone spotted her, alerted everyone, and a coordinated chant went up for her. "Hip, hip hooray! Hip, hip, hooray!" Then a beer was slapped into her hand.

Someone had wrapped Squeaky's head with a white towel and placed a shiny jewel of some sort on the front. Marie was beside her, bragging about Squeaky's past predictions that turned out to be accurate. Bonita was circling and kept coming up behind Bella and hugging her repeatedly. Despite the noise and numerous people present, Rusty refused to leave Bella's side. Numerous women talked about all the scary places they had gone looking for Bella. They discussed the feeling common to all volunteers searching for a person, which was that the world seemed too big and the chance of finding Bella had felt hopeless at the time, yet they endured.

Then they said it may have felt hopeless, but thankfully, it turned out triumphant.

Conspicuously absent was any mention of Salvia

Singleton because Robin had put the word out through the grapevine not to badmouth her.

"Where's Mom and Sofia?" Bella asked Bonita.

Bonita hesitated. "I had to make an executive decision."

Bella stared at her. "You didn't tell her, did you?"

"No, and you know why. She took care of Dad the whole time he was slowly dying. She got so depressed we thought we would lose her, then she went to a widow group and met a nice man. They left on a long cruise to South America. Even if they ruined their trip and left right away, without reservations, it would take a lot of time to get back home."

"Okay," Bella said. "What about our sister?"

"I did tell her, and she wanted to come, she really did. But I talked her out of it. She's having finals week at Michigan, and if she missed that, she would have to repeat a whole semester. She said she's praying for you constantly, and she wants you to call her."

Bella picked up the phone and dialed.

Avery, who was leaning against a wall and grinning from ear to ear, gracefully made her way through the throng of people and planted a kiss on Sandy's forehead.

Robin took a big bite of pizza. A friend spotted her and yelled, "Hey, I thought you didn't like pizza!"

Robin picked up another slice and grinned. "Pizza is celebration food, and I'm celebrating!"

❧❧❧❧

Later, Sandy headed her car toward home. Home, supposedly a place where her heart should be. But was it? Reflecting on the joy and relief on Robin and Bella's faces and then comparing it to her own dry relationship was sobering. Watching the heartfelt reunion of Robin and Bella should have caused Sandy to think about her own longtime partner, but that was not what happened. As Robin and Bella embraced, the woman who popped into Sandy's mind was Avery. Yes, Avery, whose smile seductively played about her lips. Avery, whose eyes reflected the wantonness in Sandy's own eyes.

She knew that loyalty was a good thing, but loyalty alone may not be enough. There was passion and the intimacy that naturally came with making love to a woman. Wasn't life a truly precious gift that could end at any time? And couldn't this be doubly true for a detective? Didn't she deserve the same kind of passion and happiness that Robin and Bella shared? Who was she kidding, anyway, by thinking she could have a one-time tryst with a woman who practically consumed her every thought? Sex is addictive, a wise friend of hers once said.

Sex or not, Avery or not, her problem ran deeper. She needed to exit this relationship that was devoid of sex and isolated from the intimacy of human nurturing. She needed to give herself time to find someone who would fill this void in her life.

Sandy unconsciously slowed her vehicle. She didn't relish the scene that loomed before her—of going home and pouring out her heart to Birdie. Splitting up would be painful, but she knew it was something she had to do. Anything less would be dishonest.

Once she disentangled herself, she would be free to visit Avery as an entirely different person. She would be single, unencumbered, and guilt-free. And once she made and committed herself to this decision, a weight would be lifted off her chest. How wonderful it was going to be to fall into someone's arms without guilt and the necessity of denying natural desires.

Chapter Twenty-eight: Jail Life

Monday, October 18

In Salvia's mind, the inside of the county jail was just as television portrayed it, except for leaving out the part about the attitude of the jailers. The women, at least at this facility, performed their repetitive duties like sullen teenagers, and they delegated orders like sleepwalking drones.

One woman fingerprinted her with an automated touch, a pair of women somehow managed to photograph her without falling asleep, and although their body language indicated it was obviously a huge effort, they logged in her belongings and ordered a trustee to give her a jumpsuit and rubber shoes. Salvia dressed quickly yet still noted the jailer had already grown tired of standing and waiting on her. The female jailer leaned on the wall, sighed heavily, and instructed Salvia to hurry up.

A trustee then handed Sal a frayed blanket and a thin, ratty mattress. At last, the impatient jailer was on the move again, lumbering unenthusiastically along as she escorted Salvia to the women's cellblock. The jailer's breathing was heavy and her sighs frequent until they finally reached the cellblock. There, her jailer's attitude seemed to perk up a bit, which Salvia supposed was due to the attention she was receiving for bringing in a new prisoner.

As Salvia stepped in among twenty other women,

she realized that this was the dreaded moment in the movies, where the new person was always scared half to death of the other inmates. As movies would have it, all the other inmates were going to rush up and attack the new person. But Salvia's arrival turned out to be a moment of curiosity and entertainment. The women, who were mostly young, wanted to know what Salvia was in for and how long she was liable to stay. They scrutinized her mattress, and one asked if she could trade mattresses with her just before she left since Salvia's mattress was slightly better than most.

Although Salvia half expected a den full of cruel and evil people, her reality was a cellblock full of women suffering from poverty, bad luck, and poor family ties. Most were admitted for drugs or probation violations. The women became cautious of Salvia once they found out she was booked for kidnapping and was scheduled for a psychiatric evaluation. Her cellmate, an older Black woman named Flo, said there used to be privacy about a person's charges, but with television and the newspapers, it wasn't long before all the inmates learned what people were in for. Salvia got the less desired top bunk, which was harder to get into and out of and provided no shield from bright lights. Flo warned her that most fights started in the main room where the women gathered around the TV. She said the best way to stay out of trouble was to avoid it.

❧ ❧ ❧ ❧

Salvia's main entertainment became the life drama of other women. Young women wandered in and out of their cell, visiting with Flo, dropping off the latest gossip and picking up a little advice. One thick-waisted girl often hung out in their cell. Her street name was Star, but in jail, they called her Jessie. One day, Jessie came back from a phone call bubbling with enthusiasm and adoration for someone she called Mack. Jessie claimed Mack loved her and was going to get her out soon, yet Salvia noticed Flo's lack of comment or enthusiasm. When Jessie left, Flo quietly said, "Oh, yes, those pimps are just model human beings."

To Salvia's surprise, on Jessie's next visit following a phone call to Mack, the girl came into their cell visibly afraid. She said Mack had obtained information he didn't like, "And now Mack is going to beat me!" Salvia watched with amazement because no matter what suggestions other inmates gave her, Jessie held fast to the notion that the beating was inevitable, but afterward, things would soon go back to normal.

Salvia lay on her top bunk at night with a towel over her eyes. Her thoughts revolved around how unfair life could be and how she never should have kidnapped Bella.

⁂

As her days in the county jail crept along, Salvia made a mental list of inmate injustices. She learned that toilet paper was severely limited. Any person who needed more had to buy it with their own money at the jail commissary. An unconsidered fact was that heavy women required more toilet paper, and those unable to afford it had to do without. A toothache appeared to be one of the worst afflictions. Those who suffered had to first prove they weren't faking, then get the nurse to set up an appointment with the dentist, and finally suffer until one of the dentist's infrequent visits. At a time when most dentists were advocating tooth implants and saving teeth, jail dentists routinely yanked teeth out as fast as they could pull them. Jailhouse dentistry did not require finesse or skill as much as brute strength.

❧ ❧ ❧ ❧

When she finally went to court, Salvia Singleton was found guilty by reason of temporary insanity and sentenced to six months at a state mental health facility. After listening to Bella speak, the judge had gone easy on her.

The system placed Salvia in a ward for patients with depression, where she was making tremendous progress. Although she feared her transfer to this unknown locked-down mental health facility, it too proved far less frightening than the images she had conjured in her mind. There was no shortage of little old ladies with severe depression and a handful of schizophrenics who were bounced back into lockup mainly because of a poor decision to stop taking their medication. In many cases, when a person became agitated, she noted that they began ratcheting up, and Salvia realized that, like her mother, all she had to do was avoid them.

Over time, Salvia no longer suffered from the loneliness that was once such an integral part of her life. She was even becoming personally involved with a fellow patient, a kind and gentle woman, also recovering from depression.

Throughout her stay, Salvia had one faithful and steady visitor, a woman she had come to consider an exceptionally good friend—Bella.

About the Author

Rhonda Webster lives in Denver, Colorado, with her partner, a slew of dogs, a gentle black cat, and a large flock of chickens. She is a retired nursing instructor and Colorado adventurer.

www.ingramcontent.com/pod-product-compliance
Lightning Source LLC
Chambersburg PA
CBHW031559310726
48974CB00003B/738